Written
in
Purple

By Kristen Frugé

DEFIANCE PRESS
& PUBLISHING

WRITTEN IN PURPLE

ISBN-13: 978-1-963102-49-9 (Paperback)
ISBN-13: 978-1-963102-48-2 (eBook)

Published by Defiance Press & Publishing, LLC

Bulk orders of this book may be obtained by contacting Defiance Press & Publishing, LLC. www.defiancepress.com.

Public Relations Dept. – Defiance Press & Publishing, LLC
281-581-9300

Defiance Press & Publishing, LLC
281-581-9300
info@defiancepress.com

DEDICATION

This book is dedicated to all my previous students, from elementary to high school. Every single one of you holds a special place in my heart. I sincerely hope that my work of fiction does some good for you, even if that good is as simple as giving you the courage to speak up for yourself. Never be afraid to do the right thing.

Also, I'd like to especially thank Hayden Lester, whom I taught English several years ago, for helping me with my weather-related questions for this book. Hayden is now working towards his dream of becoming a meteorologist, and has already been a part of several storm chases around the country.

PROLOGUE

The Year 2050

Robots were not exactly new, as cars could now drive themselves, but only recently had robots been introduced into society as essential workers. In some cases, it was going phenomenally well, and in others, it was not. While many people endorsed these robotic replacements, there was also, of course, a growing concern across the nation about the implications this may have for society.

One of the most hotly debated political issues was the use of robots in jobs once performed by humans. However, with the Chinese now in control of most of the world, Chinese robotics had infiltrated almost every aspect of human life in the United States of the Greater World, previously known as the United States of America. The artificial intelligence workers had already replaced most healthcare workers after new strains of the Covid virus continued to mutate and spread, along with other zoonotic diseases that mysteriously began to infect the population. While many theorized it was biological warfare, their pleas were either ignored by the apathetic or squelched by the overzealous who truly believed that the only way to save the world was to unite under a new world order.

These zealots firmly believed that Americans needed to accept the newly developed "cure," along with the deal that accompanied it. Every other major world power had already signed the treaty, they argued, loudly proclaiming all the benefits it would bring to the American people, who were dying at an alarming rate. Those who stopped to consider that there might perhaps be something deeper going on usually became infected quickly, and it became almost impossible to hide that people were purposely being infected. However, due to the chaotic state of the nation, the president at the time declared a national state of emergency, urging the American people to sign the treaty to stop the wave of death that had now wiped-out hundreds of thousands worldwide.

The Chinese scientists who developed a cure had become international heroes, and the whole world became briefly united before the outbreak of what was being called the Third World War, which had truly begun many years before with the attacks on Israel in the Middle East. The second wave of the disease, as it became known, struck the world with a vengeance a few years later. Although many Americans fought the change fiercely, the second wave mysteriously silenced thousands of the voices warning against the grave consequences of joining a world alliance and accepting a cure from China.

Finally, the inevitable happened: This generation had succeeded in convincing the next that the deals made with China would be for the good of all and America would remain the same, despite the change in name. However, the ineffectiveness of the politicians of the past in reaching any compromises whatsoever made it extremely easy for the Chinese government to force their hand in many matters once the treaty was signed.

The cure, along with the new world government, was intended to bring world peace, but in reality, it did anything but that, as the cities of America continued to be riddled with division and hatred fueled by a sadistic desire of the powerful to control the masses with fear and paranoia. Without those essential elements, the politicians' pocketbooks continuously being filled by foreign entities would cease to be filled, and their "American dream" life would cease to exist.

The rich and powerful continued to live in luxury while riots raged in the streets below. Cities such as Portland, Detroit, Chicago, and parts of New York City became almost unrecognizable due to the violence that continued to take place. The riots had become so intense that the United States president was forced to accept assistance from the Chinese yet again, and the United Nations sent highly trained Chinese mercenaries to help control the riots.

After much human life was lost, the Chinese government began mass-producing robotic soldiers to control the riots. This, of course, caused even more riots, but the success of the rioters plummeted as a seemingly endless supply of robotic troops were sent in without hesitation, causing many to simply give up any hope for change.

However, the chaos was mostly limited to the larger cities. The Southern United States still was relatively peaceful, especially Texas and Louisiana, as they had united with intent to rebel if necessary. Still, there was not much that could be done, as politics had become even more of a game of money and control than ever before; those who had claimed they would keep America great and free had mostly died out by the time these events transpired. A select few, though, still embraced the hope of America becoming a place of freedom and peace once again.

Among them were a few students attending a new school run by robots on the Gulf Coast of Southwest Louisiana, namely a young man by the name of Jason and a young computer genius by the name of Carson. These young men each knew the true history, both the good and the bad, of America. They did not want robots to take over the world, especially since the robots were controlled by China.

Everything people did was being tracked by China, and those who were noncompliant with the peace treaty were often fined in some way;

they would be caught speeding, littering, or any other small griev-ance that could easily hurt the pocketbook if it was not taken care of promptly, and once those started to pile up, one knew they were on the watch list—or even jailed. It was a sneaky and unfortunate way of con-trolling the people. Those who even so much as tried to raise gardens were often fined because of "health violations," among other things.

The America of 2050 looked nothing like the America of even 2019. The truth was that 2020 had been the catalyst for a series of unfortunate events, and this was the world in which these high school students found themselves. While parents were generally very much against robotic teachers in schools, there was not much choice left in the matter, as the human teacher shortage had become a true crisis for the youth of the nation.

The events that led up to the great teacher shortage in the early twenties had set the stage for an even greater shortage, as the increas-ingly volatile political climate hastened the decision of many to step away entirely.

During the last two decades, teachers had begun quitting at an alarming rate. This mass exodus of educators, starting with the most dedicated and qualified, caused states to create incentives to attract new, unsuspecting teachers. These newcomers often came running into the proverbial fires of education with all the hopes and dreams of changing the world, only to be left with unrealistic expectations weighing so heavily on them that they could not bear the brunt of the burden. They escaped the flames encumbered by a host of medical issues, including anxiety, depression, and a wide range of physical ailments.

The low pay, lack of substitutes, and lack of understanding of the real needs of students from those in power caused this teacher shortage to become a full-blown national crisis. In the year 2040, after many debates and struggles, the controversial trial of the robotic teacher program was initiated in every state in America. Every school district was to have a test run of this trial, but the actual implementation and guidelines took another ten years to map out.

Technology had advanced by leaps and bounds, and despite World War III being in full force, the program began. The initiative was meant to be a trial run for all school districts, but one school from each district would be selected to participate and the first two years would be voluntary, although everyone knew that meant it was eventually going to be mandatory. Parents could choose but were encouraged to sign up their children for this new, innovative school. The initiative read as follows:

- **In order to create a learning environment that ensures absolute accuracy and efficiency for young learners, we have replaced teachers with artificial intelligence agents that will answer every question in every subject imaginable. These state-of-the-art robots are designed to appear human but will wear the same professional attire daily, eliminating any need for dress code complaints aimed at teachers. These robots are programmed to monitor and video every angle of the classroom in order to do what humans cannot: be everywhere at once. If a student is falling asleep, the robot will alert the student to raise their head and pay attention. The robot also will simultaneously monitor every website the children visit during their learning experience and promptly shut down any non-educational websites or off-task programs. This will enhance learning and increase test scores in low-performing schools. The program has already succeeded in several schools nationwide, producing higher scoring schools in ninety percent of the participating schools.**

- **If a student is noncompliant, the robot will document and** record the behavior in an objective manner. If the student continues to be noncompliant, the robot will alert the security robot to escort the student to administration. Administration will consist of several human components to ensure oversight of the robots. As such, undesirable behaviors should be minimized, instructional time will be maximized, and test scores should improve.

- The social-emotional component of your child's education has always been a priority. Therefore, the robotic teachers are specially trained to detect your child's emotional well-being and send them to a human or robotic counselor when appropriate. You will sign a form at the beginning of the year to determine if you prefer a human or nonhuman (android) counselor. The robots will be referred to as Teacher (Name), as they are genderless, which is the preference for much of society.

- The benefits of these robots are vast. In addition, this will ensure the children do not form emotionally inappropriate bonds with their teacher or vice versa, and it will help eliminate the human component of error in carrying out fair and equal discipline.

- As these robots are very expensive, any student who causes intentional damage will be required to replace and pay for the parts necessary to repair the robot. Students also will be subject to suspension or expulsion for violence against the robots.

- Robots will also monitor school bathrooms. Though these robots will not be equipped with cameras, they will have the power to detect suspicious substances and alert security robots.

- Robots will grade students' work in a timely manner and will never lose an assignment. Robots also can detect if a child is lying about anything and are able to determine exactly what is needed to enhance each student's learning.

• Replacing human teachers is cost-effective and will save money in the long term, as robots will invariably produce more efficient learning techniques than humans. The robots also will be able to detect if a child is sick or using a pretense to avoid working, diagnose the child quickly, and alert the parents in an emergency. Nurse robots are trained in CPR as well as other medical procedures that may be necessary in an emergency.

CHAPTER 1

ROBOTICS READINESS HIGH

The Year 2050
Southwest Louisiana

Humidity hung in the air as the very first students to enter the new high school program began to arrive. Jessica, a senior with long blonde hair, looked at her friend Alicia and rolled her eyes as the new robot duty teacher welcomed them to school.

"Good morning, Jessica. Good morning, Alicia. My name is Teacher Denise, the duty teacher." The robot paused and moved its head to the side slightly in a deceitfully humanlike manner. "I detect cynicism. Please adjust your attitude," the robot said in a matter-of-fact tone.

"*You* adjust your attitude," snapped Alicia.

Laughter ensued from the group of students gathered in close proximity. "Alicia, I detect anger. That is understandable; this is the first day of a new year. Can I assist you in finding your first class?" the robot asked calmly.

Alicia and Jessica stared at the robot as more students passed them, basically ignoring Teacher Denise as the robot identified itself.

"I cannot believe my parents are sending me to this stupid school. I thought human teachers were dumb, but this is even stupider. Except I bet we'll be able to get by with anything! What can a robot actually do to us anyway?" Jessica laughed.

"No robot's gonna do anything to me," said Jason, another senior, a football player with a large attitude and a snarky mouth.

"Please find your first-hour class," announced the robot voice over the intercom. It may have been pure curiosity that overtook them, but interestingly, the students did indeed move to their first classes of the day.

Class Room 34

In the first class of the day in Room 34, the students filed into the classroom as they chatted, each one greeted by their robotic teacher. Not one name was mispronounced, and not one student was overlooked. There was no need for a roll call; the robot was programmed to recognize each student and mark absent anyone who did not appear before the first bell rang.

"Good morning, class," said the robot. While they were designed to be genderless, this one resembled a biological woman, complete with a modern but uncontroversial outfit. The robotic teacher appeared so real that the students were a bit flabbergasted. They had been expecting machines, not these uncannily humanlike beings. Even though they had been able to tour the school before the semester began, the students had not officially met the robotic teachers.

"My name is Teacher Oxford. I will be your English teacher this year. Please find your assigned seats."

"We have assigned seats?" asked Haley, a tall thin girl with green eyes and heavy makeup. "Seriously?"

"Yes. I have assigned your seats based on a large database of information regarding your best social-emotional match as well as your best academic match." The human-like robot responded.

"Are you a boy robot or a girl robot?" asked Jason.

"I am neither. I am genderless as to help you focus on your studies."

"You sure look like a girl robot," he commented, pointing to certain aspects of the robot's build.

"Jason, that is not an appropriate comment or gesture. That will be one strike in your behavior log," Teacher Oxford replied.

With a motion so natural that it stunned the students, Teacher Oxford motioned for the class to sit. "Estimated time wasted on useless questions ... five minutes. Off task ... educational priority rerouting. Please open your devices and turn to lesson one. Shakespeare is our first topic."

A little stunned at the abruptness of the robot, the class of fifteen seniors moved to comply, partly out of curiosity, and many of them opened their devices to the first lesson. Some did not, though, and decided that they would much rather watch the entertainment portion of TunedIN, previously known as TikTok.

"Haley, Marcus, Joanie—you all have one behavior strike. You will now be rerouted to the correct website to ensure you are on task."

"You know, I've had about enough of you, Teacher Oxford," Jason piped up.

Teacher Oxford slowly turned to Jason but promptly responded, "Jason, that's behavior strike number two. Your final warning will be the third one, at which point you will be escorted out of the room. You have wasted approximately one more minute of instructional time. "Documentation taking place . . . Marley, please pick up your head; you are not allowed to sleep. My calculations detect that you did not receive adequate rest last night. However, you may not sleep in class. You are wasting your education. Five more minutes of instructional time has been lost. Please turn to lesson one of Shakespeare's classic play Hamlet."

As the lesson began, the students continued to try various ways to test the boundaries with the novel teacher robot. Marcus, a smaller boy with a sneaky personality, attempted to throw a spitball at Teacher Oxford. As he shot it at his target, Teacher Oxford moved its arm in the middle of the lesson and promptly caught the spitball with the speed and precision only a robot could possess.

Amazed and a little frightened, the students' eyes widened waiting to see what would transpire next.

"Marcus, that's behavior strike one. Human saliva detected in paper scrap," said the robotic instructor.

"It's called a spitball!" Jason smirked.

"How do you know that was me?" Marcus argued.

Teacher Oxford immediately projected video footage of Marcus forming and aiming the spitball for the students to see. Silence filled the classroom.

"Now, let's continue. Approximately ten minutes of instructional time have been lost so far in this class. The more instructional time is lost, the longer you must stay after school to compensate for the lost time, as per the handbook. Any more interruptions will result in even longer makeup instructional time."

The lesson went smoothly for approximately five minutes afterwards. However, the first day of school is the day students like to test boundaries, robots or no robots.

In fact, the robotic teachers were likely to be tested even more than a human teacher, as the students overall thought the entire program was a joke; it was mostly parents and educational bureaucrats touting the program. They would receive a hefty bonus if the initiative worked, and a heavy fine if it failed.

The robotic teacher's explanation of necessary class materials was interrupted by the telltale flash of someone snapping a photo. "No cellular devices are allowed in the classroom without permission. Return your phone to its designated stowaway area or else it will be confiscated," Teacher Oxford stated.

"What are you going to do about it?" asked Carson, the culprit. "I mean, you're a robot. I was taking a picture of my first day of robot school."

"Carson, please come forward and surrender your device if you refuse to comply."

"Seriously, what are you going to do about it?" Carson laughed as the rest of the class giggled nervously. "I bet I could hack into your robot system and shut you down anyway."

Immediately following Carson's statement, a loud alarm screeched, "Security threat. Activate safety protocol."

The doors to the classroom slammed shut, and bars resembling those of a jail cell slammed down over the windows.

Teacher Oxford calmly walked to the corner of the room and stepped into the robot charging station, complete with bulletproof, hackproof walls.

"What is happening?" Jessica asked, eyes wide.

"This is insane! LET US OUT!" Haley screamed.

"Everyone, remain calm; this is standard protocol for a security breach. Instructor threats will be taken seriously. The security team will be in within the next five minutes," Teacher Oxford's voice echoed from the charging station.

"This is the stupidest thing ever," Jason said as he stood up and walked toward the door, fully intending to try to kick it down. He let out a string of expletives as he did so, only to be reprimanded; Teacher Oxford's voice warned Jason that his inappropriate language was not tolerable and that he would be considered a security threat if he tried anything.

Jason, however, was furious. He'd really had enough of the "robotic nonsense," as he called it. He was not a particularly large young man, but he was strong, and when he was angry his strength surprised even the most intimidating opponents.

"You can't lock us all up in here with no good reason! We got rights, or we used to! I'm gonna kick down the door. Y'all ready?" he asked, swaggering to the door, his lanky frame exuding confidence.

"Please just sit down! You're going to get us in more trouble!" begged a timid girl in the back.

"I ain't putting up with anymore of this nonsense!" With the force he usually put behind his tackles in his football games, Jason attempted to body slam the door. Unfortunately, the moment he chose to storm the door was the same moment it opened for the security robots.

Classroom 32

In the freshman social studies class, things were going a little more smoothly—until the security alarm went off, terrifying the freshmen and making them antsy. The robotic teacher attempted to continue the lesson despite the disturbance.

Their teacher was named Teacher Phil. Teacher Phil was programmed to be a quieter robot with a calm demeanor, and although they were all supposed to appear genderless, he appeared to be male and had a deep, low, yet still robotic voice. As far as technology had come, it was challenging to completely imitate a human voice, as tone and cadence were difficult to replicate.

"Class, the security alert is only for your safety. It is a Code One. This means that an instructor was threatened. The security team will take care of it promptly. Please remain calm. Lessons will continue as scheduled in other classrooms."

"I'm scared—why did the bars go down on the windows?" asked a petite blonde sitting in the middle of the classroom.

"It's okay, Marella," the girl next to her by the name of Raine responded. "It's just a safety precaution. Remember? That was part of why our parents wanted us here. It's supposed to be the safest school because of how quickly the instructors can detect and respond to threats. I'm sure it will be handled."

"Thank you, Raine, for assuring your peer of their safety. Your behavior has been noted as positive," Teacher Phil's robotic voice echoed through the room. "Now, restructuring for on-task behavior. During the period known as the American Revolution, a man named Thomas Jefferson wrote an important document agreed upon by all the Founding Fathers of the nation. Please direct your attention to your devices to see your next task, which will be annotating and deciphering ideas in the Declaration of Independence. While this is an antiquated document, as we have since rewritten the Constitution, you will be ana-lyzing the ideas that led to the need for change. You will then answer a series of questions that will display on your screen to determine your depth of understanding."

Although there were several students whose parents had strong feelings about the topic of the rewritten American Constitution, they dared not voice their opinions, seeing as they were already in a security threat situation.

"This is kind of cool," whispered Charlie, a mischievous boy with blond curls and an eccentric sense of humor. "I kinda like robot teachers."

"Charlie, I am pleased with your assessment, but we prefer the term 'instructors,' as robotic teachers is impersonal. In addition, please do not speak unless you have something of value to add to the lesson."

Charlie stared at Teacher Phil for a long time, not sure what to think.

Room 34

The door to Room 34 swung open just as Jason charged, resulting in Jason colliding head-on with the security robots. Unfortunately for Jason, the security robots were extremely sturdy. Although he'd absorbed thousands of tackles over his years as a football player, his body was no match for the cold steely robots. He collapsed onto the floor, resulting in yet another alert.

"Medical emergency—student unconscious. Please step to the side." One security robot began assessing Jason's vital signs, determining he would be fine. However, the other honed in on Carson instead.

"Carson, you have been designated a security threat. Jason also has been designated as a threat, but he is currently unconscious. He will be informed when he regains consciousness."

"No duh, he's unconscious," snapped Alicia. "Because you made a huge deal out of nothing!"

"All security threats to instructors will be taken seriously. The first offense will result in a suspension. When Jason regains consciousness, he will be escorted to the office and informed of his punishment. Carson, please come with us." said one of the robotic security guards.

At this point, Carson decided compliance was his best course of action, but in his mind he began to formulate a plan. He knew his parents would be furious with him, and thus he also knew he would need time before executing what he thought would be the most effective way of eliminating this strange new world.

The alarms soon subsided, and the class grew quiet after an outburst from the girls, who were terrified. The bars slowly crept up and revealed the sunlight behind the windows. Carson went willingly with the security robots, glancing down at Jason with concern.

"Will he be okay?" Carson asked. "I'm sorry, I didn't mean to cause a disruption." The young man decided to play along for now. "I definitely didn't want Jason to get hurt—I think he was just trying to help me. Does he have to get in trouble, too?" he added.

"Come with us. Jason will be handled according to protocol. Apology accepted. However, you will be disciplined according to the handbook. You are still deemed a security threat due to your comments," Security Robot 1 stated. "Your apology has been documented. We sense a change in your demeanor; your heart rate has slowed, and you are now thinking logically. Compliance will be considered. Continued compliance will result in a more positive outcome."

"Thank you." Carson smiled and winked at his classmates slyly.

The robots somehow missed that, but they did not. His peers received the message clearly and seemed to decide as one to follow his lead. While robots could detect many things, deciphering nonverbal social cues was still one precious commodity humanity possessed.

Jason was starting to stir, and when he did, he was still furious.

"Jason, it's okay. Just trust me, okay?" Carson said as he was being escorted out.

"That freaking hurt," Jason grunted. "Isn't there some law against that?"

"Jason, you may have suffered a mild concussion. However, you attempted to escape during a threat. You must come with us to the office after you have visited the nurse again," said Security Robot 2.

"Teacher Oxford, it is safe to exit your security enclosure," added Security Robot 1.

"Wait, what? Where am I?" Jason asked. He may have been short-tempered, but he was also extremely intelligent, having caught on to his best friend Carson's plan without a word being spoken. In the past, he would have argued and taken the consequences from a human, but he was smart enough to know this situation would require a bit of a different approach.

CHAPTER 2

PUNISHMENT AND PLANS

Carson and Jason were escorted down the halls by the security robots to the principal's office once Jason had been assessed by the nurse. The principal was human, but she supported the robotic initiative and firmly believed it would work. Therefore, the boys knew their best shot would be to attempt to do what they had always done best before: charm humans. Jason was particularly charismatic, while Carson had a reputation as generally being a good student.

Mrs. Leichenberg, despite her small stature, could command a room and terrify anyone with a simple look. Her short blonde bob outlined her weathered face, making her appear even more stern than the robots.

"Good morning, Officer Reginald and Officer Ronald." She nodded to the robots.

So they had names, too, Carson noticed. Jason also took note and added it to his mental notes, although his head still pounded from colliding with their unforgiving frames.

"Carson, Jason, have a seat," she stated calmly, though she was clearly seething. "What happened?"

"Well, we were just making jokes and that ... English teacher decided to take it seriously." Jason couldn't help but make a snide remark from the start.

Carson eyed him with a look that reminded him to be on his best behavior.

"Really?" Mrs. Leichenberg said, looking doubtful. "Show me the incident."

"Initiating sequence of events after transfer from Teacher Oxford," said Reginald, the first security robot.

"Teacher Oxford, pardon the interruption. Please send a video file of the events from the morning," Ronald's robotic voice droned.

"One moment, please," the reply came back from Teacher Oxford in record speed, and with not a moment of class time lost.

"Please project the events, Ronald," Mrs. Leichenberg requested.

Ronald lifted his arm as it transformed from a human limb into its robotic counterpart to assist in projecting the scenario.

Mrs. Leichenberg watched the scene, frowning and eyeing the boys. She winced a little when Jason was knocked to the ground, and Jason saw that as an opportunity to play on her heartstrings—something he could not do with robots. He only hoped it would work.

Leichenberg was known to be cruel and coldhearted; she had come from another school run by humans with a reputation for being erratic, but had somehow been able to procure this job that required a great deal of handling people and machines. She herself was a master of manipulation, though. Those who knew who she really was had been baffled when she took this position, but she currently had everyone believing she was an incredible person with great skill.

In reality, she lacked in many areas and had been fortunate not to be fired from her previous job. She had explained her way out of the bad reputation that tried to follow her, and somehow all of it had been believed. Had it been robots hiring her, she may not have been able to convince them so easily, but for now robots were only employees, not administrators or anyone in charge of the staffing for schools.

"Carson, your words could indeed be considered a threat, but I do think that perhaps the alert was a bit of an overreaction. However, our policy is that any and all verbal threats will be taken seriously and will result in an in-school suspension," Mrs. Leichenberg finally stated.

"Threat level has been assessed to be minimal. Please make note," she added, looking at the security robots.

"Noted. Carson Myers has been assessed as a minimal threat. Behavior modification will be an in-school suspension," Reginald's voice echoed.

"We will have to contact your parents, Carson," Mrs. Leichenberg added. "Now, on to your behavior, Jason."

"Well, I was just a little freaked out about the bars on the windows," Jason lamented. He decided to play the sympathy angle, or at least try to do so.

"Jason, we know your track record very well. You cannot seriously tell me someone who brought an alligator to school as a prank was scared of that," Leichenberg quipped.

"But that was an animal! I'm not used to machines. It's a little unsettling," Jason continued to work his magic. "Besides, you weren't even here that year—it's just a stupid thing that's followed me since ninth grade. It was just a little alligator, and it didn't hurt anyone."

"I know, and it was my fault for making a stupid comment," Carson added. The boys glanced at each other, the unspoken plan continuing to unfold.

"But Jason," Carson added, "that alligator wasn't *that* little. It was at least four feet long, and it scared me a bit! You're lucky they didn't send you to jail for it since that is a huge violation of safety."

"I detect deceit," Ronald stated. "The fear of alligators is not detected in either of the subjects when they discuss the animals. Their heart rates remain the same."

"How can you detect deceit? You're a freaking robot!" Jason snapped, letting his temper get the best of him yet again as he slammed his hand down on the desk in front of him. Carson shot him a warning glance.

"We prefer the term 'nonhuman instructors,' or simply our names," Ronald replied. "I detect fear."

"I ain't scared of you," Jason continued. "I'm mad at you because you railroaded me!"

"Jason! That's enough!" Mrs. Leichenberg shouted.

"Mrs. Leichenberg, please lower your voice—we detect anger directed toward a student. Anger will not adequately modify behavior. You must readjust your methods. Jason, you are upset. Take a moment to calm down," Reginald, the first security robot, droned.

"Hey, that thing is actually right for a change," Jason laughed.

Mrs. Leichenberg's temper rose, but she managed to compose herself. She gave the robotic security a stare that would have pierced the soul of a human being; however, robots were only able to detect physical cues to assess situations, and the look meant nothing to Ronald or Reginald. Their only means of assessment was the ability to read pulse rates, voice tones, perspiration levels, and other factors that would indicate the demeanor of a human.

"Jason, first of all, I will calmly address the fact that you were disrespectful to Teacher Oxford with your comments."

"Disrespectful?! This is the dumbest thing ever," Jason snapped. "It isn't a person!" Carson continued to move his head in an attempt to redirect Jason, but Jason just couldn't seem to restrain himself.

"Jason! You will stop it right this minute. You are being ridiculous!" Leichenberg snapped back, exasperated.

"Mrs. Leichenberg, you will not be allowed to call a student names. Please apologize. We will deal with the behavior and respond accordingly," Reginald stated.

Jason grinned. In that moment he realized he'd discovered a gold mine of manipulation, and he understood what Carson's plan must be. They had been friends for many years, and despite being very different, they often could understand what the other was thinking.

"I'm so sorry, Mrs. Leichenberg," Jason said. "I lost my temper, and I should not have said that. Officer Reginald, Officer Ronald, I do apologize. This school has always had a vendetta against me since I brought an alligator to school in ninth grade. They never forgave me, and it's clear this new principal is just trying to get me in trouble for something I did in the past, and I'm just trying my best. You can access my grades and see I'm pretty smart."

The robots could not detect manipulation quite like a human; thus, they sided with Jason. "Apology accepted, Jason. We detect sincerity, as your comments indeed match the level of Mrs. Leichenberg's blood pressure. Her vital signs indicate that she is indeed angry in your presence," Ronald stated in a robotic voice.

Jason and Carson grinned at each other.

Mrs. Leichenberg's face was as red as the fire extinguisher hanging beside the door, and her arm hair stood on end. She could see that Jason was trying to trap her, as she was aware of his past antics and had been warned that this was one student she may have trouble handling. This made her feel all the more insecure, as she knew deep down inside that her ability to handle people—or lack thereof—was the very reason she was stuck running a robotic school. She had been exceedingly fortunate that her political views and her elderly relative on the school board's money had secured her the position.

She stared at the two boys with disgust as she responded to the robot's reprimand. "Jason still must account for his behavior today. Jason, why did you try to escape during a security threat? You are not allowed to leave the room during an emergency, and you know that."

Leichenberg was still visibly fuming but had managed to lower her voice.

"I was just afraid, and my head hurts now." Jason thought of his most intense football game in order to raise his blood pressure artificially, hoping the robots would detect his anxiety.

"We detect rising anxiety in Jason," Reginald assessed. "I recommend allowing him to rest in the nurse's office before continuing this conversation."

"I assure you he's fine," Mrs. Leichenberg argued, raising her voice to a thunderous yell.

"Mrs. Leichenberg, you are the administrator, but our assessments are based on data, not emotions. Therefore, on my authority, I will escort Jason back to the nurse's office for assessment. His behavior will be dealt with whenever he is physically able to relax."

Jason smirked at Mrs. Leichenberg and winked at Carson as Reginald escorted him out of the room.

"Now, Carson, we will be contacting your parents," Mrs. Leichenberg stated. "However, I need to make an announcement to assure the student population that the threat is no longer active."

She cleared her throat as she activated the PA system. "Attention, students of RRH: The threat has passed. Your classmates are safe and being taken care of accordingly. Please resume your normal activities."

Nurse's Office

The robotic nurse, accompanied by a human nurse in the event of robotic malfunction, assessed Jason.

"Jason, your blood pressure is elevated, and we know you suffered a mild concussion," Kandy, the human nurse, stated. "Why don't you lie down for a bit, and we'll call your parents to come and get you?"

"Please, I feel awful," Jason said, rubbing his head theatrically.

"Assessment valid. Noted," Nurse Callie, the robotic nurse, added. "You also require adequate hydration. Please drink this water."

Jason complied, drank the water, and kicked back on the table to rest until his parents were contacted. He grinned when the robotic nurse turned away, thinking about how he and Carson would carry out their unspoken plan.

CHAPTER 3

STUDENT REACTIONS

Room 34

Unsure of what else to do, the students complied with the remainder of the lesson. Carson returned to class shortly after and participated fully in class. He knew his suspension would begin tomorrow, along with Jason's. For now, he kept his plan tucked safely in the back of his mind until he could find more allies.

His parents had been furious when they received the call, but also a little unnerved about the incident, and they had considered pulling him from the school. Carson had begged to stay, which they had found odd. However, in his mind the best course of action was to stay in the midst of the chaos and expose the robotic teacher initiative for exactly what he believed it was: ineffective and dangerous.

An announcement came over the loudspeaker once more, this time a curious one. "Attention, all personnel not currently teaching a class, please report to security for a brief meeting. Pardon the interruption."

The students eyed each other suspiciously.

"I'm sure it's just for safety precautions. I apologize I caused an incident," Carson said after gaining permission to speak.

"Thank you for the apology, Carson. Your remarks have been

noted. Thank you for assuring your classmates of their continued safety. Safety is the first priority here at RRH, followed by your educational and social-emotional needs," Teacher Oxford replied.

Carson sighed. He was not exactly thrilled about being in this school, of course, but he saw no other alternative to help others from meeting the same fate as him and his classmates. As much as they had complained about their human teachers, the students certainly missed having a real person to talk to, even though they'd all been raised around robotic devices.

Human connection could not be recreated with a device, and while society had been attempting to prove otherwise for years, the evidence that it didn't work only became more tangible daily. These robotic teachers were only a physical manifestation of a broken society, one on the brink of imploding on itself.

Room 32

The announcement for all personnel not teaching a class had slightly surprised the class of freshman, but they had continued to follow their robotic teacher's instructions. When it came time for group work, though, problems arose.

"Class, it is time to move into groups. We have grouped you according to your specific skills, personalities, and scores. We have used data to determine the best fit for you. Group one is as follows: Charlie, Raine, Jazmeena, and Dante."

"Sweet!" said Jazmeena. "I like my group."

"Jazmeena, please refrain from making comments while instructions are being given. You will be given a warning mark for disruptive behavior. Estimated time lost for correction and interruption: one minute. Documentation occurring," Teacher Phil droned.

"Seriously?" asked a mouthy girl named Blaize. "We've never had a teacher mark us for being excited about a group assignment before."

"Blaize, please refrain from making comments when instructions are being given. You will be given a warning mark for disruptive behavior. Estimated time lost for correction and interruption: one minute. Documentation occurring," the robot repeated.

"Wait, didn't you just say that exact same thing to Jazmeena?" asked Charlie, his bright-blue eyes lighting up with mischief. He saw a golden opportunity. "Hey, guys, watch this ..."

"Charlie, please refrain from making comments when instructions are being given. You will be given a warning mark for disruptive behavior. Estimated time lost for correction and interruption: one minute. Documentation occurring."

Charlie beamed, and his classmates caught on quickly. The entire hour was spent disrupting Teacher Phil, but because Teacher Phil was programmed to immediately respond to disruptions with documentation, he had no other choice but to continue repeating himself for the next several disruptions. The entire class erupted in laughter every time it happened.

Unfortunately, some students did not understand that after so many disruptions they would be sent to the office, and Dante was the first to receive enough behavior marks for an office referral. Teacher Phil had repeated his documentation phrase three different times to Dante, but each time with an escalating consequence. Dante had not noticed this, however, because he had only been interrupting every now and then.

"Dante, that is your final behavior mark for disruptions. You will now report to the principal's office for further redirection. Do not resist, or we will call in our security escorts to ensure you arrive at your destination."

"He sounds like that old device our parents talk about called Siri," laughed Raine.

"Raine, please refrain from making comments when instructions are being given. You will be given a third mark for disruptive behavior. Estimated time lost for correction and interruption: one minute. Documentation occurring." Teacher Phil turned toward Dante. "Dante, report to the office, or you will be escorted by security. Estimated time for compliance: one minute."

Fearing what may happen, Dante complied, walking out of the room and heading for the principal's office.

This particular group of freshmen possessed a keen intellect, and by now they had realized how many times they could interrupt class before being sent to the office. Therefore, the ones who had not interrupted yet chimed in, and those who only had one warning took turns interrupting. This routine amused them greatly, as a human teacher would have been beyond frustrated at this point and would have also been able to redirect the class effectively.

The laughter became so loud that the next classroom over, which happened to be Teacher Oxford's, appeared on the smart board.

"Is there a need for assistance in Classroom 32?" Teacher Oxford asked. "Please lower your voices. You are interfering with learning in Classroom 34."

The freshman class howled with laughter, and while the senior class next door found it amusing, they had just witnessed one of their classmates receive a concussion and bars slam down over the windows. They were hesitant to make a sound and instead followed Carson's lead of silence.

"Noted," Teacher Phil replied. "Assistance is not necessary. Behavior marks are being given; disruptive students are sent to the office on the fourth offense. One such student has complied." The robot turned to his students. "Class, your volume is too loud. Lower your voices or you will all receive another disruption mark."

The freshman quieted down after seeing the senior's glares through the screen, and Carson winked at them. They all admired Carson's brilliance, and they knew they could trust him. "Hey, where's Jason?" Charlie asked.

Teacher Phil droned out his warning speech.

"Jason's whereabouts are not your concern. He is safe," Teacher Oxford said. "Estimated time lost due to external interruption: five minutes. Disruption noted. One strike for Teacher Phil has been added to your profile. Do you need further assistance?"

"No further assistance is needed," Teacher Phil replied.

"Do you accept the strike on your profile?" Teacher Oxford asked.

"Strike accepted. Disruptions have exceeded the limit for the class period. Thank you."

The students' eyes widened, wondering what a strike meant for the robotic teachers. They were genuinely fascinated and became determined that next week, when their behavior slate was refreshed, they would find a brand-new way to get another strike against their strange new teacher.

However, all the students seemed to have forgotten that any minutes they lost in class were required to be made up at another time. The freshman had wasted an entire class period, but they were having too much fun to remember or care.

The bell rang.

"You are dismissed to your next class. No running or horseplay in the hallways; the hall monitors will record any instances of behavior issues in the halls. There are no monitors in the bathrooms for your privacy, but a monitor will be outside the bathrooms to detect any suspicious activity that may require intervention. Have a nice day," Teacher Phil said.

In Teacher Oxford's class, the same announcement was made before students started filtering out of the room.

CHAPTER 4

THE FURY OF JAMIE FONTENOT

"*We are committed to keeping Robotics Readiness High a safe campus.*"

Both Carson's and Jason's parents were notified of the incident immediately, and due to Jason's injuries, Jason's mother soon arrived at the school to figure out exactly what had happened. She was not pleased and entered the front office quite agitated.

"May I help you?" asked the secretarial robot through the intercom, surrounded by thick barred walls.

"I'm Jamie Fontenot, Jason's mother. Let me in to see my child! What in the world happened?" she demanded.

"Mrs. Fonteenot"—the robot mispronounced the name, as unlike the instructor robots that had been specifically programmed to pronounce student names correctly, this robot had been overlooked for that task—"please lower your voice. Your access will be granted upon the decrease of your pulse. I detect high pulse rates that could cause irrational behavior. Student safety is of utmost priority."

"Is it?!" she fumed. "Is it really? If it was, I wouldn't be here to see if my baby is okay! This is supposed to be a good school, and it was one of the few left allowing football programs, but instead he gets a concussion from one of your stupid teachers?! I need to be let in IMMEDIATELY... and my name is isn't Fon-*tee*-not. It's Fontenot.

Get it right! I demand to see someone human *now!*"

"Security threat possibility at the front door," Sandra, the robotic secretary, droned.

"*You're* the security threat!" Jamie snapped. "Let me see my baby! Where is this new Leichenberg person?"

"Thank you, Sandra. I'll handle it." Mrs. Leichenberg appeared at the window.

"I detect threatening behavior," Sandra noted to Leichenberg.

"I will determine that," Leichenberg snapped at the robot. Sandra, unlike a human, did not respond in any manner other than what was expected from a robotic device. "Do you want to override precautionary measures?"

"YES!" Leichenberg yelled. "I just want to talk to this parent."

"Mrs. Leichenberg, please lower your voice—blood pressure rise detected. This will not be helpful or professional in handling challenging situations," Sandra added.

Mrs. Leichenberg's face turned red, and Jamie Fontenot howled with laughter. "Oh, see, now they got you, too, huh? My husband and I argued for days about if this was the right school for Jason, and well, I'm not so sure it is, but this is freaking hilarious."

Leichenberg's face oozed anger and contempt, but she knew she had to behave in front of the robotic secretary. "There are not many other choices, and without special permission, you would not have been granted access to this school," Leichenberg said condescendingly.

Jamie Fontenot just looked at her, still amused from the previous interaction with the robot. She awaited another clever quip, but none came.

"Mrs. Fon-tee-not," Sandra chimed in. "Your blood pressure has decreased to suitable levels. You are now permitted entrance. Threat no longer valid."

Leichenberg fumed internally, but managed to compose herself as Jamie Fontenot walked past Sandra.

"Good morning. Sandra, is it?" Jamie said. "I trust you will maintain the safety of the school?"

"Good morning. We are committed to keeping Robotics Readiness High a safe campus," the robot answered.

"Good, good. Well, now I'll have a word with Mrs. Leichenberg, and if you detect her anger and blood pressure rising, you'll let me know and protect me?" Jamie asked. Had a human been on the receiving end of this communication, the human would have picked up on the social cues revealing great sarcasm and amusement.

"We are committed to keeping Robotics Readiness High a safe campus. Do you feel threatened, Mrs. Fon-tee-not?"

"No, not right now, but if I am, I'll let you know." Jamie grinned and followed a beet-red Mrs. Leichenberg into her office. "Where is Jason?" she asked.

"He's resting in the nurse's office for now," Leichenberg answered. "However, we need to talk about the behavior that led to this incident."

"No kidding," Jamie snapped.

"Jason violated protocol. Please play the video footage, Security Officer Reginald."

The incident was projected from the robot's vest into the air.

"Wow," Jamie said. "Just wow. So, you're saying you wouldn't curse and freak out if you were a kid who'd just been locked in their classroom over something that stupid?"

"Mrs. Fontenot, we have a strict no-tolerance policy on swearing, and violating safety protocol is even worse. It could have put everyone in danger," Leichenberg replied, regaining some of her composure. "He does not seem to understand the seriousness of his offenses. These teachers are expensive and far superior to humans, who are prone to error in the classroom."

"Sounds like the kid was making a joke and that robot didn't understand it. And I don't believe for one minute that robots are better than humans." Jamie rolled her eyes.

"We prefer the term 'instructors,'" Reginald chimed in.

"Oh, do you, now? Well, I prefer my seventeen-year-old son not to have a concussion right before football season!" Jamie fumed.

"Mrs. Fontenot, please lower your voice. We detect elevated stress levels," Reginald responded.

"Well, at least this one got my name right," she laughed. "Of course I'm stressed! This is about my child! I fear for his safety after all this."

"We are committed to keeping Robotics Readiness High a safe campus," Reginald stated, parroting what Sandra had said when asked about safety.

"So, what happens next?" Jamie asked.

"Jason will be suspended for two days. It's an in-school suspension," Mrs. Leichenberg responded.

"Who will be supervising this?" Jamie asked.

"One of our instructors, of course." Leichenberg replied condescendingly.

"So, more robots? Ugh, David is going to hear about this later. I have half a mind to just pull Jason from this school today, football program or not!" Jamie sighed, exasperated.

"Well, that's ultimately your decision," Leichenberg answered calmly. "He does have a record of behavior issues. Remember, once he's removed he cannot be reinstated, and he will have another record following him for the rest of his life."

"Y'all are still hounding him about that stupid alligator incident as a freshman? You don't even know Jason, or this town, or anything about this area!" Jamie snapped.

"We keep extensive files on each student in order to better understand their personality," Leichenberg responded.

"Files only give you data, and data doesn't show you the person behind those behaviors. But you wouldn't understand that here at robot school, would you?" She sighed in frustration. "I'm worried, and I want to see my son now!"

"Sensing concern. Please allow Mrs. Fontenot to see her son," Reginald said.

"But I'm not finished yet!" Leichenberg barked.

"Mrs. Leichenberg, continued noncompliance in socially distressing situations will result in negative consequences for both you and the school," Reginald stated.

Jamie's face lit up. Her son had inherited her unique genius, and she was starting to understand how to play the game, too. "Thank you, Reginald. Or is it Officer Reginald, or Instructor Reginald?"

"Officer Reginald is my name. Thank you for your cooperation."

"She isn't cooperating, though, she's using you!" the principal snapped.

"Mrs. Leichenberg, that is one strike. Undermining the assessment of school authority is a serious offense," Reginald droned.

Leichenberg's face lit up with rage, but she remained silent, knowing her mouth just might be the end of her career if she did not learn to play by these strange new rules. While she was also a manipulative person, she had no practice manipulating robots, and they were much more difficult to manipulate than people. After all, she had used her political views as well as her cousin, a local lawyer, to manipulate the decision to hire her—but there hadn't been that many candidates wanting the job in the first place, so she hadn't had much competition.

"Please come with me, Mrs. Fontenot." Reginald stood up and held out his robot arm to show her the way.

"Thank you." She smiled. "I do appreciate it, and thank you for listening to my concerns."

"We are committed to addressing your concerns here at Robotics Readiness High," Reginald repeated the overused phrase with a slight variation to match the comment.

Jamie knew then exactly what she had to do if her son was going to graduate, and while she wished with all her heart that his father was not so adamant on Jason's placement at this school, she knew his chances of getting a scholarship were slim to none if he transferred. Robotics were the future, and having gone to a robotics high school would ensure acceptance into a good college and a good career trajectory.

She also still wanted him to play football, although American football had suffered a fierce decline since the immense changes in the strange new world. Previously known as Lakeside High, Robotics Readiness High had been one of the few schools in the area to retain a football program, which was part of what had attracted parents to actually consider giving the robotics program a chance. What they didn't know was that it was all part of a ploy to retain those parents and children who would otherwise be skeptical, though some, like Jamie Fontenot, remained skeptical, nonetheless.

Jamie's thoughts were interrupted as Officer Reginald pointed the way to the nurse's office where Jason awaited.

Nurse Callie and Kandy greeted Jamie as she approached.

"How is Jason?" she asked.

"Hey, Mama," Jason said, sitting up quickly only to start falling back.

"Jason, you suffered a mild concussion. No sudden movements," Nurse Callie admonished.

"Well, at least some of the robots have sense here," Jamie scoffed. "Are you okay, son?"

"Yes, ma'am. Did they tell you what happened?" Nurse Kandy asked.

"Yes, and we'll deal with that later. I think they overreacted, but it's whatever. Your dad is so set on you staying here to play football." She sighed.

"I want to stay," he said, thinking of the look he had shared with Carson and the plan they had formed silently to expose the school for exactly what it was in his mind: a failure.

"You do?" Jamie looked surprised. "Well, we'll talk about that when you don't have a concussion. Do you realize that you just injured one of the star football players right before the season started?" she asked, turning to look at both the human and the robot nurse.

"I'm sure he'll recover quickly," Kandy, the human nurse, replied. "I've seen worse from football injuries."

"Chances of long-term injury are minimal in comparison with football injury risk. Additionally, football is not the main focus at Robotics Readiness High," Nurse Callie added.

"Injury during a security drill can be minimized by complying with established procedures."

"Oh, there it is." Jamie rolled her eyes. "There's the robot part of you. I should have known... come on, Jason, I'll take you home and you can come back tomorrow. Sounds like you're suspended, but we'll see how that goes before we decide if you're coming back for good or not. Is it okay if I go check him out now?"

"You are free to go," Nurse Callie said. "However, the student must return for suspension or fines may accrue for parental figures."

Jamie rolled her eyes, ignoring the last threat from the robotic nurse. She had argued with enough machines for the day.

"Mrs. Kandy?" she asked. "I prefer to speak to a person."

"Yes, that's fine," Kandy responded. "Just make sure he gets rest and stays hydrated. Bring him to the ER if he experiences any further symptoms."

"Oh, if he experiences any further symptoms, this school may have a *huge* lawsuit on its hands," Jamie said snarkily. "The ER isn't going to help much, either, because it's just those same dumb machines running it."

"Lawsuit threats are not taken lightly here at Robotics Readiness High. You must have a valid reason to sue a school. Additionally, the ER is the safest place to bring a student if symptoms worsen," Nurse Callie droned.

"Oh, shut up, you big bucket of bolts," Jamie said as she and Jason walked out of the nurse's office to check out at the front.

Carson's parents, however, had quite the opposite reaction to Jamie Fontenot. Carson Mire came from a very progressive family, even for the times they were living in; they had supported all of the government programs similar to the robotic teacher program, and they valued what they considered to be peaceful alternatives to conflict. Thus, they were very upset with Carson, but they dazzled the instructors as much as you could dazzle a machine that wasn't quite human.

They remained calm, spoke with respect, and—while it frustrated Mrs. Leichenberg beyond belief—they wanted to know the root cause of what would have made Carson feel the need to say that. Mrs. Leichenberg's raging response gained her another strike from Reginald, as she had fumed that sometimes kids are "just stupid." Meanwhile, Reginald praised the Mires's calmness and cooperation and added them to a list of "trusted parents" stored in a database somewhere. Even Mrs. Leichenberg hadn't known about this list, and she was completely taken aback by the whole interaction.

It was agreed that Carson would serve his suspension, and he also was in deep trouble at home; his parents decided he would lose access to his electronics unless they were needed for school. Carson realized this was going to halt his plan of action considerably, but he also knew he needed to bide his time until he could really figure out how to execute his ingenious plan. For now, he would simply have to wait, and at some point he'd have to tell Jason all about it.

CHAPTER 5

HEROES OR VILLAINS?

S everal weeks passed without much further incident, save the occasional angry parent interaction resembling the one with Jamie Fontenot. Some students were pulled out of the school, while most remained except for one student who had been expelled within the first week. Routines were established, and while it was nothing at all like the school they once knew, as humans were known to do, the students adapted.

There were several students who remained simply because of the sports program. Parents like the Fontenots missed the old America, where football was a fundamental part of Friday nights, voting wasn't a charade, and China didn't control everything. They did their best to teach their children about the America they vaguely remembered, but it had changed so much after the second pandemic altered everything.

Meanwhile, Carson and Jason decided to formulate their plan carefully after school one bright fall afternoon in the parking lot of a local abandoned fuel station. Most of the fuel stations had been replaced by electric car chargers, and in protest, some people in the community had begun riding horses to school and to the store until the local government outlawed horses as a form of transportation. That was a bitter battle that still raged on, as many still blatantly ignored the law, arguing it was their constitutional right. The local law enforcement, however, argued that the Constitution had been rewritten in the year 2030 to reflect a more progressive America, and hence that was an invalid reason. A horse strode by with a single rider as they sat there talking.

"So, what's the plan?" asked Jason. "We need a plan, and I know you've got one."

"First, let's make sure no one's listening," Carson said as he pulled out his tiny phone from his pocket. "Hey, phone, go incognito," he instructed.

"Are you sure you want to go incognito?" the automated voice asked.

"Yes." Carson replied.

"Incognito feature disabled by the carrier," came the reply from the little cellular device.

"Dang it," Carson said. "My parents."

"Hmmm. What if we just 'lost' our phones for a little while?" Jason asked. "They probably heard you say that. It's like we get no privacy anymore."

"Yeah, I wonder... what was it like in the world when you could just disappear with no one knowing?" Jason asked. "I wonder sometimes. My dad talks about it a lot, how America used to be a lot different for his parents, and then his generation ruined it."

"Careful, they'll hear you on the phone and think you're being unpatriotic, or not accepting other cultures or something. You know how they get," Carson warned.

The "they" he spoke of was the newly formed local government that really had nothing to do with the American justice system; it was more of a universal patrol system that was used everywhere. It had, of course, come with the trade with China to procure the cure for the second pandemic. Many things had been sacrificed in an attempt to save the citizens of the great nation now known as the United States of the Greater World.

"So, what are we going to do? How are we going to talk about this?" Jason asked. Carson motioned for Jason to watch, then put his phone down and walked about fifty feet away. Jason followed.

"There, I think that's probably good. Dude, really?" Carson asked, pointing at Jason's phone.

"Oh, my bad!" Jason sprinted over and put his phone down, returning quickly. "So, what's the deal? How do we fight this?"

"Well, first of all, we're going to have to make sure none of our conversations are overheard while we do this thing. And when I say 'do this thing,' I want you to know that it could go one of two ways: we could be the heroes, or we could end up in jail. You understand that?"

"Yes, I got it. I want to do something. We can't just sit back and let the world be as stupid as it is! I want that world back that my dad talks about," Jason said. "Back when you could do stupid stuff without every detail of your life being recorded and broadcast and held against you. Back when people had the freedom to say stuff without worrying about their phones reporting them."

"You sure, man? I'm going to feel horrible if it ends badly," Carson said.

"I'm sure. Never been more sure of anything in my life." Jason responded, nodding in agreement.

"Now, first things first. If we're gonna take down the robotic regime, you are gonna have to remain calm and not go around bulldozing robots. Think you can do it?" Carson asked.

"Yeah, man, I can do that. I'll keep it cool," Jason assured him.

"Alright, then. Here's the plan…" Carson started.

CHAPTER 6

FLAGS ON THE PLAY

Football had been in full swing for a few weeks, but a surprise awaited the team at practice one hot September day following a rough Thursday night game that had resulted in several players being injured. The football program still was run by a human coach—the only exception to the robotic instructors besides the principal. The coach had been fed up with the robots for some time now, but he had desired to stay and coach because he had graduated from the school long ago, back when it was Lakeside High School.

The Lakeside mascot had been a gator—that had been part of the joke when Jason brought a live alligator to school years ago. Coach Hoffner was a tough man, and he had led the Gators to many state play-offs. One year, they had even won the state championship. However, since the advent of robots, sports had become a hotly debated subject, making coaching a risky career.

Sports were seen as frivolous by many schools, and the once central role that sports and athletics played had been replaced by tech-ready program initiatives. The money that used to feed athletic departments now went to tech classes, and the robotics lab homed the new jocks. To be on the robotics team was now the ultimate honor, and the football jocks were no longer the popular students they once had been many years ago. Anyone who remembered the years before the second

51

pandemic could attest to the vast difference between going to school then and now. The old movies showcasing football players as stars were antiquated and puzzling to most students, but a few die-hard fans like the Fontenot family held fast to the belief that football and good old American tradition would make a comeback.

Jason often struggled with this, as he had secretly wanted to be on the robotics team for the popularity, yes, but also for the knowledge. It certainly would have come in handy in the predicament he and Carson found themselves in currently. Despite this, Jason had decided to still dedicate his time and effort to football, but this particular day made him so angry that he had a difficult time maintaining control. He knew he must, though, or he'd never be able to help Carson carry out his plan.

"Alright, guys, listen up!" Coach Hoffner hollered. "There's been some changes, and I don't like it any more than you're going to like it."

"Negative school talk is not permitted," Assistant Coach Randy stated.

"That was not negative school talk," Coach Hoffner snapped, his blood pressure rising. He had struggled with this new environment all semester and had fought hard against having a robotic assistant coach in the first place. The school district had insisted, though, citing safety concerns and the fact that he would have a greater ability to protect himself from lawsuits or slander if he had a robot documenting his every move.

"Anyway, because of all the injuries last night—some pretty serious; let's keep Jalen in our prayers as he recovers—"

"Expressions of religion are strictly prohibited," Coach Randy interrupted.

Coach Hoffner cursed, inciting Coach Randy correct him once again.

"Due to all the injuries, the district has decided that—because of a suggestion from ol' Randy here—we are going to only be playing with flags, no tackling. Flag football will be the only way we can play. It's supposed to keep you safer." He scoffed as he finished.

A chorus of complaints and protests arose from the boys.

"Flags?! Are you freaking serious? This is ridiculous!" Jason shouted. "Flags! All because someone got hurt? How about we ban robots since, you know, that's what gave me a concussion? Why don't you wear a flag, Randy Dandy?"

"Jason, that is one strike on your behavior log. Suspension pending if you continue," Coach Randy stated. "You already have one suspension. Two more will result in expulsion."

"I'd like to expel something, alright," Jason muttered, but it wasn't loud enough for the robot to pick up. He then made a noise with his arm that sounded like flatulence. Loud laughter erupted from the rest of the players following his comment, along with other boys imitating his behavior. Randy remained unmoved; the robotic instructors had not been programmed to understand that this was a distraction.

"Do you need to use the restroom?" Randy droned, resulting in even more uproarious laughter from the team.

"Yeah, I do . . . oh my!" Jason cried, making even louder noises with his arm. "Must have been those beans we had for lunch."

Coach Hoffner shrugged and rolled his eyes. "Jason, pipe down. We'll talk about it later."

"Contact with students outside of school hours is strictly forbidden," Coach Randy interjected.

"Bruh, shut up!" Evan, a freshman, chimed in.

"Evan, that is one behavior strike for you as well," Randy noted.

Coach Hoffner motioned for the boys to knock it off, and they complied. No one paid much mind to the robotic coaching assistant after that and the team continued with practice without further incident, despite having to learn how to play with flags instead of physical contact.

Chapter 7

Upcoming Storms

Carson and Jason met daily after school to work out their plan, though it truly wasn't much of a plan yet. They were becoming more discouraged day by day as the ever-increasing invasion of privacy and dictatorial demands of the instructors continued to evoke chaos. The app once known as TikTok, now called TunedIN, was now society's main source of news. Journalism and news reporting as Generation Z and the now elderly millennials remembered it was a thing of the past. TunedIN was where people went to see the news, weather reports, and whatever else the government wanted them to read.

However, it was highly censored, and while other apps that still held to the value of free speech would arise, they were always fined out of existence or would mysteriously get "bugs" and infect the phones and devices of everyone who utilized them. This was what had first planted the original idea in Carson's head—to fight fire with fire, so to speak.

Successfully hacking into highly secure systems like those of the robotic instructors, though—and doing it without getting caught—was highly improbable. And yet, it seemed like the only way to stop things from continuing to spiral downward.

Carson had been reading many books on such topics that had been long since banned in schools. He had found them in a pile of trash one day while looking for robotic parts and simply taken them home and started learning more about how the world was before the pandemics struck. While the book ban was not strictly enforced outside of schools, reading a banned book was enough to land you on a watch list. So, he avoided this by taking a page or two outside after reading them and feeding them to his recycling robot prototype he had been working on. Each day as he destroyed more pages, he would test the various ways it could dispose of the trash more efficiently, but despite their destruction, Carson remembered the information they had contained and kept shorthand notes hidden in his room.

Over time, he had learned what to do and say to avoid potentially being put on a watch list. Carson had a vast knowledge of how technology worked, resulting in his ability to type just the right thing into his search bar that wouldn't raise a red flag and result in fines or unnecessary attention. He was a cunning kid, and he freely shared his knowledge with Jason. Jason was a bright kid in his own right, but he didn't always understand Carson's reasoning. He had learned, however, to trust Carson's instincts, as he was usually accurate in his assessments.

The sky was a bright blue and filled with large puffy white clouds as Jason and Carson met at their usual spot and abandoned their phones. Today, though, a surprise awaited them: a girl with long dark hair was sitting there reading a book that Carson immediately recognized as one that would quickly put you on the watch list. She sat reading against a tree, not a phone in sight at first glance.

Jason's face lit up, and Carson knew what that meant. He tried to motion for Jason to just ignore the girl, but he also was curious simply because of the book she held.

"Hey, you new around here?" Jason asked, swaggering up to the girl. She looked up from her book, her dark-green eyes half annoyed, half curious.

"Yes," she said, then continued reading.

Jason, accustomed to girls being very pleased to speak with him, was taken aback. "Hey, those are ugly shoes," he said, trying to get a reaction out of her.

"Really?" she responded flatly. "I don't care what you think. They're vintage. They're called Hey Dudes, and hey, dude, why are you bothering me?" The girl giggled a little at her own quip as she stared down at her flowery pink shoes.

"I'm Carson," Carson interjected. "Sorry about him—I don't know what's wrong with him sometimes. How did you find that book?"

"I do not wish to discuss that with you," she said, eyes darting around as if looking for devices, becoming visibly nervous. "I'm not even supposed to be out here alone, but I have to get away from the nonstop monitoring sometimes."

Carson noticed a phone resting on a branch high up the tree.

"You may wanna put that somewhere further away if you're trying to avoid being seen and heard." Carson looked at the branch where it sat, wondering how in the world she had gotten it up there.

"Oh my," she said. "You think? I thought it was far enough out of range."

"Eh, you may want to rethink that, Katniss," Carson said, pointing to her book.

"Hey, you know *The Hunger Games?*" she asked, her eyes lighting up.

"*The Hunger Games?*" Jason piped up. "Hey, my dad talked about a teacher he had years ago who loved those books! She was a millennial—she's probably ancient by now, but Dad really liked her as a teacher. He said she quit, though... I don't know, something about purple ink or her ideas being too radical or something. I don't even think he knew all of what happened, but he knew she cared about her students. She did some weird crap, though. She loved cheese, too, and he said something about rats, but I don't know what that had to do with it. I wasn't listening the whole time Dad was rambling. He does that sometimes—"

"Wait, what was her name?!" the girl interrupted to ask.

"Mrs. Thibodeaux."

"Oh yeah, she was my dad's teacher, too," Carson recalled. "He just was talking about that year when we looked at his yearbook recently. He said he felt bad about messing with her—he mentioned rats falling from the ceiling or something like that. They put a fake rat in her desk once. She was a great sport, but then it made the principal mad she didn't punish them or something. Other than her calling my dad Max instead of Dax all the time on accident, he said he liked her okay."

"Well, surprise, I happen to know her very well. In fact, she's in town right now visiting family," the girl replied.

"How do you know?" Jason asked.

"She's my grandma."

"Whoa, hold up—what's your name?" Jason's eyebrows raised.

"Princess. I'm named after a character from some old show about zombies or something … I don't know. My parents are kinda weird, but I love them. My dad's name is Micah."

"Whoa, small world," Carson said.

"Wait, your grandma is in town right now?" Jason asked. "Like, the Mrs. Thibodeaux who ate cheese all the time and loved all the weird old books?"

"Yes. But she isn't weird—she refers to herself as 'quirky.' She's actually super against this whole robot thing, and she came here when she heard about my cousins going to that school. I… probably shouldn't say anymore."

"Wait! Her grandkids go there? How did we not know this?" Carson asked.

"Well, Charlie is her grandkid. Her daughter—my aunt—married some boy from down here named Charlie Robert McGinnis, but the rest of the family is still in Texas. She's hoping to move to Alaska. She says they're still pretty free up there, despite everything. Or Mexico—there's some really desolate places out there."

"I really would be careful," Carson cautioned, again eyeing the phone propped precariously on the branch overhead.

"Oh yeah, I have it on incognito. That's just a precaution." She grinned.

"Hmm, I may like you after all." Jason grinned back and winked at her.

Princess rolled her eyes. "We came down here to help them evacuate from the big storm," she added.

"Oh yeah, that thing is coming in a week or so, huh?" Jason remembered. "I don't know what we're going to do yet. Those dang robots keep telling us to remain calm."

"Hey, what are they going to do with all those robots while we evacuate?" Carson asked.

"I heard they were transporting most of them all to a safe undisclosed location as soon as they end school on Tuesday," Princess responded. "The storm isn't supposed to hit until next Friday or Saturday." After a moment, she asked, "So, what are you two doing out here anyway?"

"Uh… well…" Jason began, eyeing Carson.

"I think it's okay, Jason. First, let me ask you, Princess—what do you think of that book?"

"Oh, this book is great. I wish that society had realized it was a commentary on where things were headed. I mean, we're not exactly like that, but in many ways, we've come close. I'd say that our society—other than literally throwing kids into an arena—is reminiscent of the one the author depicts."

"Oh, big fancy words!" Jason said with a smile. "You must be a Thibodeaux. That's the other thing she did, used big fancy words—or so I hear. Every once in a while, my dad will use one of those fancy words he learned from her."

"Alright. Well, our phones are way over there. Are you sure yours is incognito?" Carson asked. "It actually isn't even a real phone, but I didn't want to tell you that in case you were dangerous. Clearly you're not, though," she said. "I left my real one at my aunt's house and grabbed a toy since I wanted them to think I had some way to contact others. I'm leaving this book here, though. I found it in the field, and I've read it before. I just wanted to get away and happened to see it." Princess closed her book and looked up at them.

"So, what's the deal? What are y'all plotting?" she asked, looking at them intently.

"Okay, so here's what we were thinking…" Carson began to detail his plan, but just a few moments later, a robotic officer came walking up to them.

"State your objectives," the robotic voice said.

"We're just hanging out," Carson replied.

"Your cellular devices indicate they are out of range. Your parents are concerned. Please return to your homes immediately."

"We can't ever get away from you people!" Jason snapped. "Except you aren't even people!" Carson and Princess both shot him looks of warning. Princess quietly hid her book behind her back.

"Please show your hands," the robot warned Princess upon detecting her movement. Princess showed her empty hands. "Detecting rising heart rate and cause for suspicion. Please rise."

"She isn't doing anything wrong! Leave her alone," Jason said as he stepped in front of her, feeling a powerful protective urge rising up within him.

"It's okay, Jason," Princess said, standing up. The book was gone. Jason looked surprised.

"Jason, you, um… didn't exactly win the last battle you had with a robot," Carson reminded him softly.

"Please refer to me as Officer Grady," the robot stated. "You will treat authority with respect and return to your dwellings."

"Okay, okay," Princess agreed.

"Analyzing data—you are not a citizen of this town. Please state your business."

"Visiting family. Storm evacuation preparation, sir," Princess responded militantly.

"Best wishes, and know that your safety is our top priority. Please return to your designated visiting residence at once in order to prevent harm."

"Okay, I'm leaving." Princess winked at Jason and Carson as she walked off, the outline of a book clearly visible under her shirt that was now tucked in to just the back of her pants. Jason howled with laughter, causing Grady to question him.

"I'm just nervous," he quickly tried to save face.

"Noted. I detect attraction to the female to be a factor in poor judgment," Grady stated.

"Bruh, no privacy?!" Jason muttered, glad that Princess was out of earshot.

Carson couldn't help but laugh despite Jason's glare. "She is pretty, Jason."

"Weird," Jason stated, "but yeah, I guess. It's whatever. I definitely don't need some robot spouting out all my business, though, even if I did think that!"

"Please refer to me as Officer Grady," the robot said again. "Retrieve your cellular devices. You will continue to be tracked until arrival at your home is safely documented."

"My word...okay," Jason complied. "Hey, come to our game Friday night!" he added, yelling to Princess. "I'm number sixty-three! It's flags, but I might accidentally run into someone, and it'll be exciting!"

The two boys parted ways, deciding they would find another time to discuss things. As they walked home, both were still fascinated by the interesting new girl they had met in the field.

CHAPTER 8

PROTESTS, RACISM, AND OTHER FORBIDDEN TOPICS

S chool continued to be a challenge for the next several days. The boys continued meeting with Princess, knowing school would be dismissed for the arrival of the upcoming storm within a few days. Robotics Readiness High would be dismissed earlier than other schools due to the robotic teachers having to be transported to a safe location. In the meantime, however, the robots continued to be a source of anguish for parents and students alike.

Teacher Phil had one strike against him, and now the students were curious to see what exactly would happen if he got another one. The freshmen had not tried anything in a while, not after they had witnessed other students get suspended over minor infractions or misunderstandings. They continued to be well-behaved, for the most part, in Room 32. However, Charlie couldn't help but be a bit mischievous at times.

That day, the students were learning about the riots that happened after the second pandemic and were encouraged to talk in groups about why those riots had occurred and how to avoid becoming part of a protest. Protests led only to people getting hurt, Teacher Phil explained. "These protests started out as peaceful. But there is no such thing as a peaceful protest. Protests inevitably lead to violent riots, and that is why they are prohibited in the new Constitution. Please discuss with your groups. What is your question, Charlie?" Teacher Phil responded to Charlie's upraised hand.

"Well, couldn't you have a peaceful protest?" Charlie asked. "I mean, couldn't you change things like that?"

"Protests are always illegal, and protests cannot be peaceful. They always turn violent. Data supports this," Teacher Phil responded. "Please discuss with your groups."

"What data? Can I see the numbers?" Charlie pushed. "Was there ever a peaceful protest that worked? Why do we learn about Rosa Parks and Martin Luther King Jr. and stuff if peaceful protests don't work?"

"Our data indicates that different time periods require different actions. Their actions would not work in our current time period, and we now know exactly how to carry out social justice; therefore, there would be no need. Racial tension is a thing of the past, as is any type of division in society. We have eliminated all disparity and eliminated the need for protests of any kind," Teacher Phil responded.

"Except it still does exist," said Dante, who often felt the very real tension as he moved through the world due to being African American.

"Data shows that we have eliminated all factors that would cause division," Teacher Phil responded.

"Hmmm… wait till I tell that to my mama," Dante replied.

"Instructors will not tolerate student threats to report false information to their parental figures," Teacher Phil replied. "One mark."

"For telling the truth? This is— "Dante began, only to be given another mark.

"He's right, you know," Charlie added. "I still hear of people being hateful to other races or other groups of people. It's not gone."

"Charlie, that is one strike."

The class then erupted into a chaotic argument, some siding with Teacher Phil, some with Charlie.

"My mom said that things were way worse back in the day," Raine said calmly.

"Well, you haven't lived in our shoes a day in your life!" Dante yelled back.

"He's right," a young girl named Talia said quietly. "Jewish people also have suffered many injustices that would not have been solved without protests."

"I think you're all missing the point—there was a rebellion. It was a rebellion of people, and people rebelled!" Timothy, a boy who loved to steer the class off topic, interjected.

"Timmy, that has nothing to do with *anything!*" Marella, the quiet girl, spoke up. Chatter, yelling, and heated arguments continued.

"Class, you must remain quiet. Refocus your attention," Teacher Phil commanded.

The class ignored him.

"Teacher Phil," a voice came over the loudspeaker moments later.

"Teacher Phil responding."

"Teacher Phil, please note your class is out of control. You will receive another strike. The next will be your final strike," the robotic voice stated. "Do you accept this strike?"

"I accept," Teacher Phil responded. "Estimated instructional time lost: ten minutes. Class, refocus. Recalibrate."

"But we're discussing what you wanted. You just don't like our answers," Charlie said snidely.

"Charlie, that is your second strike."

"I just don't understand it," he said. "Why do you not want to talk about it? Aren't we supposed to be learning history?"

"Charlie, that is strike three. Additionally, please refer to the class as 'social studies.' 'History' has religious overtones and may be considered offensive."

"What?" Charlie looked confused.

"Charlie, report to the office," Teacher Phil stated. "You have reached your third strike. Attention, Principal Leichenberg—sending student to office per discipline policy."

"Alright, send them down," she responded over her intercom.

Another voice followed. "Teacher Phil, please report to the disciplinary office. This is your third strike, as behavior in your classroom is still not under control. Do you accept this strike and understand its implications?"

"Yes, I understand." Teacher Phil said methodically, and without emotion.

"We will send in a replacement to cover your class. Please remain where you are until you are relieved."

"What's gonna happen to him?" Dante asked, wide-eyed.

Charlie called out as he left the room, "Y'all let me know what happens!" The boy was much more interested in what would happen to Teacher Phil than he was upset about being sent to the office.

CHAPTER 9

LEICHENBERG'S LOWERING

In the office, Mrs. Leichenberg sat across from him, her face red with anger. "Charlie, that's the second time this year you've been in here. What did you do now? What is wrong with you little punks?! You think you're so great because you have all these newfangled gadgets? Well, you should be glad it isn't like the old days," she started to lecture.

"Mrs. Leichenberg, that is your second warning this year. Please lower your voice. You must treat students with dignity and respect during disciplinary actions," Officer Reginald stated calmly.

"I'm too busy for all this nonsense!" she shouted. "Request to disable Officer Reginald."

"Request denied. Reginald has not broken protocol—you have. Two more strikes and you will be escorted out, Mrs. Leichenberg," Officer Ronald replied.

Leichenberg seethed, while Charlie grinned. "Thank you. I felt unsafe."

"Safety is our first priority here at Robotics Readiness High," Officer Reginald and Ronald droned almost simultaneously.

Leichenberg was furious but managed to calm down a bit. "Please play the sequence of events," she requested.

After seeing what Charlie had done, she again began to lecture Charlie about the importance of respect and how stupid he was for asking those questions. However, she was immediately reprimanded sharply for calling him names and reminded that she had only one strike remaining. "I have never seen such ridiculous and spoiled kids," she muttered.

"The children are not spoiled. They appear perfectly healthy," Officer Reginald stated.

"Not that kind of spoiled! Ugh…why did I want to work with robots? I have enough going on without this!"

"Mrs. Leichenberg, please use the terms 'officers' and 'teachers' instead of 'robots.'"

Charlie beamed with glee watching this interaction unfold.

"We have been observing your interactions with students, and based on our data, this is a repeated issue. You continue to undermine the robotic staff in front of students, and you call students names and raise your voice. This does not align with the school discipline plan. Please remember to be professional, or we will remove you immediately and replace you with a better fit."

"You can't do that if I unplug your sorry self," she snapped.

"Mrs. Leichenberg, that is strike three. Please gather your things and leave the premises."

"NO!" she yelled. "I will not! I'm calling the district! This is insane—you need a person during a crisis like the hurricane that's coming up. You cannot do this with just robots!"

Charlie said, "Does this mean I can go?"

Officer Reginald replied, "Yes, please return to class until further notice. Your discipline will be handled after this situation is resolved."

"Situation?! *You're* a situation!" she screamed.

Charlie did not often have much pity for Leichenberg, as she was a terrible person in general, but today he actually felt a bit sorry for her. He had struggled with the same sentiment toward the machines.

"Are you gonna be okay, Mrs. Leichenberg?" he asked as he got up.

"I would've been if it weren't for you stupid kids that caused this! You people don't even know how to behave for robots—good luck finding a *human* to teach you!"

Any feelings of pity Charlie had evaporated quickly as he darted out of the office, ready to be out of the path of her wrath.

Students switching classes gathered around to watch as Mrs. Leichenberg was escorted off campus. They were instructed to return to their classes, though, and an announcement came on the loudspeaker about an hour later.

"Attention, RRH. There has been a change in leadership. Due to the unstable nature of humans, we have replaced Mrs. Leichenberg with an instructor whom you will refer to as Principal Peterson. He will better carry out the school's discipline plan. Any student who has a complaint about Mrs. Leichenberg is encouraged to talk to Counselor Helen, and she will determine if further action is needed. Thank you for your patience. Please resume learning."

CHAPTER 10

FRIDAY NIGHT LIGHTS

The phone call announcing the change in leadership elicited varying responses from the parents. With the upcoming storm, most were too distracted to be too upset about the change in leadership within the school. Some chose to keep their kids home until after the storm, while others were actually a bit relieved that the cruel Mrs. Leichenberg had been relieved of her duties. It was not without incident, though, as she then began filing complaints and doing her best to regain her position at RRH.

The school also reminded parents of the football game happening the following night, which would be the last school event before the impending storm expected to make landfall within a few days. Hurricane Camden was predicted to be an unprecedented storm,

registering wind speeds of 160 mph at the time of the mass phone call. Its current trajectory was the well-beaten path that hurricanes often traveled, with Southwest Louisiana in the bull's-eye. Even with all the novel changes to government and society, the threat of a hurricane remained something that united communities in a way that only those who have lived through such an event would understand.

On that night, though, the community came together to enjoy one last football game. The parents had been furious about the transition to flag football, but that change had also come right before the storm news, making the flags seem insignificant. Interestingly, the boys had all agreed it was fine for now and had asked to remain at the school despite the strange transition. Jason—known to be quite convincing and charming—had talked to all of his teammates, assuring them that if they could stick it out just a little longer, change was coming. He was able to insinuate that a plan was underway without alerting the robotic staff. Since his incident with the security robots, he had become quite an expert at talking in a way they would not understand.

Tonight, Jason's adrenaline was pumping because he knew after the game, he and Carson—along with Princess—would continue their plan to make the world right again. Though ambitious, it was a plan that took advantage of the upcoming storm. Things could either go very well, or they could take a sinister downturn, but Jason lived for the thrill of being under pressure, which was part of what made him such an incredible football player. He played many other sports as well but football, despite his lean stature, was his passion. Before the exile of contact football, Jason had often taken down guys three times his size, much to everyone's amazement. He was smart, fast, and passionate—exactly the kind of personality Carson needed to help implement his plan to save the school from artificial intelligence.

The stadium was full of fans cheering, as well as crawling with robotic security guards. Coach Hoffner and his assistant prepared the boys for the first game of the season with only flags, warning them what would happen if they violated the no-contact rule on purpose.

"But what if we accidentally run into someone? We'll be running, because you *have* to run," Charlie asked with a laugh.

"Please make every effort to remain safe and avoid physical contact in order to ensure no penalties are imposed," Assistant Coach Randy droned.

"I wish I could shut that one off," muttered Coach Hoffner.

The boys smirked, and some laughed nervously.

"Please repeat your statement, Coach Hoffner. Did not compute," Assistant Coach Randy responded.

"I just said we gonna win this football game!" Coach Hoffner replied, realizing he had a chance to redeem himself. His heavy Cajun accent often caused confusion for the robotic assistant anyway, and as usual, Coach Randy did not understand most of what he said.

"The Robotics Readiness High football team has a twenty-five percent chance of a win tonight after calculating team statistics versus the other team's statistics."

"Stats don't measure heart!" Joseph Jackson, one of the sophomores, yelled.

"YEAH! JoJo, JoJo!" they all started affectionately chanting Joseph's nickname.

"Please reserve your enthusiasm and energy for the playing field," Assistant Randy stated.

The boys howled even more after that, Coach Hoffner laughing right along with them.

For a no-contact sport imposition, there was certainly lots of back-slapping and harmless horseplay in the locker room for the next few minutes.

"JoJo, get your gear on, it's almost time. And quit slapping people with your shirt!" Coach Hoffner bellowed. "It's game time! Y'all ready?"

More loudness ensued as the Robotics Readiness High football team pranced out with their flags on. Jason took the opportunity to rip his flags off and wave them in the air over his head as he ran out, causing the older cheerleaders to roll their eyes and the younger ones to cheer and holler his name.

The rest of the team followed suit behind Jason until Coach Hoffner motioned for them to cut it out and put the flags back on. Half the stadium had a good laugh, while the other half had the same reaction as the older cheerleaders. A couple of parents yelled their boys' names until the announcements came over the loudspeaker:

"Parents and students of Robotics Readiness High School, please remember you represent your school tonight. If there are any more distractions from the players from tonight's game, suspension or other consequences WILL be given."

To the surprise of the parents and students, the voice booming across the field was a familiar one: Mrs. Leichenberg.

"Also, any parents or students that had a part in the uprising that caused a leadership change will be handled AFTER the storm. The phone call you received yesterday was in error. I will resume my duties here as principal, and I WILL be respected."

"NOOOOO!" a chorus of students moaned along with a few angry parents. The stadium was slowly becoming an angry mob of people arguing on the home team's side.

After about ten minutes of confusion and shouting, another announcement came.

"Attention fans," a robotic voice began, "please make your way back to your vehicles or designated transportation hubs. Due to unrest in the stands and a risk of potential harm, we will be canceling tonight's game. Please return home and continue your preparations for the upcoming storm."

"What the heck?!" Jason yelled. He tossed his helmet down angrily. "Not like I need a stupid helmet when it isn't even *tackle* football!"

"Jason!" Carson heard his name being called from the stands.

Coach Hoffner motioned for the boys to go back to the locker room. "I'll handle this, boys. That Leichenberg woman is something else...I don't know how she managed to bribe robots, but I won't stand for her stealing even more of your high school football experience. These stupid flags were already beyond enough! WHERE IS LEICHENBERG?"

"Please remain calm, Coach Hoffner. Mrs. Leichenberg can be located near the concession stands. Do you request an exact location? Is it an emergency?" Assistant Coach Randy asked.

"Yes, it's a dadgum emergency! I have had enough of them taking away our freedoms, and now they're taking the best part of high school away from these boys!" Coach Hoffner fumed.

"Location detected. Here are the coordinates." Assistant Coach Randy complied.

In the midst of the outburst from Coach Hoffner and Jason, Carson had been adamantly trying to signal Jason from the stands. Jason finally realized what was going on and threw down his flags to go see what Carson needed.

"Come on, let's get out of here!" Carson said. "This is the perfect chance to have a quiet conversation about our plan. They'll be too distracted trying to stop the riot—we just have to blend in."

"Okay, sure," Jason agreed. He started to follow Carson, but then he realized Carson was not alone. "What's she doing here?" he asked, completely forgetting he had invited Princess to the game.

"Hello to you, too. I'm trying to help y'all not have to deal with nonsense. You're welcome, flag boy." Princess snapped back playfully.

"Alright, cool it, you two," Carson said. "We don't have time for you to be arguing about everything. She can help us. She has an idea."

The three teens slipped unnoticed under the bleachers, as the security robots were on high alert in the midst of the football field, which had quickly turned into an even more chaotic scene. Coach Hoffner and a host of angry parents had found Leichenberg, blaming her for the cancellation of the game, and they also began threatening the robotic staff, causing a host of security breaches. Loud alerts, beeps, and sirens blared through the night. Jason, Carson, and Princess were able to make it to the back of the school grounds without being noticed since most of the robotic staff were controlling the football arena. However, they had forgotten about the perimeter guards.

"Please return to your designated area. This is not a drill. Security threat level enhanced," the guard stated.

"They, they...they threatened us! Please let us get away. We need to get home!" Princess panted, thinking fast of a way to distract the robotic guard.

"Where are your parents? Locating parents for ...state your name."

Princess winked at the boys and gave the name of another student she knew.

"Oh no, there was a threat to the security guard! I heard it at the field. Someone is coming!" Carson yelled. "You better get to your robot safe place—"

"Security threat noted," the guard said, but did not move.

"He's not kidding—look, listen to TunedIN," Jason said, pulling out his phone to show the robot live coverage of the chaotic football field.

"Processing threat...threat is valid, but one must protect the young children before entering the safety chamber," the guard stated.

"Oh, like the one that charged me?" Jason's adrenaline levels rapidly increased.

"Just run!" Princess said. "There's three of us—he can't chase us all."

"I'll meet y'all where we first met! I'm gonna run home and grab a change of clothes first," Jason said.

The three took off in different directions, and Jason, thinking fast, placed several large sticks in the path of the security robot.

"Attention: All school security robotic personnel needed on the football field immediately. Threat has escalated."

The robot turned and ran toward the football field, obeying its new orders.

CHAPTER 11

GRANDMAS AND GATORS

About an hour later, the three teens met under the tree where they had first met Princess. "Alright, do y'all have your phones?" asked Carson.

"Yes," said Jason and Princess.

"Hey, listen," Jason urged.

All three phones blared an alert as TunedIN popped up. The headline read "Riot at Robotics Readiness High."

"Oh no! That's Coach in handcuffs!" Jason exclaimed.

"Hahaha, and Leichenberg right beside him!" Carson laughed.

"Oh no, my dad!" Jason screamed, looking closer at his phone. "My dad! They've got my dad! And my mom!" Jamie Fontenot was also in handcuffs, but she was fighting mad, as was David Fontenot, her husband.

"Oh no, my parents are calling," Carson said. "Hello?"

"Carson, where are you? Why are you in the middle of nowhere? Are you okay? I'm sure they can come to a peaceful resolution. I hate that this is happening," Dax Mire, Carson's father, said.

"Dad, I…can't explain right now, but I'll be home in a little while. I'm okay. If my phone goes off, well, security threat and all, but I'm okay." Carson hesitantly hung up the phone.

"Great!" Princess yelled as Carson hung up.

"Yeah, now they know where we are!" Jason screamed. "What's wrong with you?" He pushed Carson a little.

"Look, man, I know your parents are in handcuffs, but think about mine, too. They need to know I'm okay! Nobody's going to be okay if you don't help us with this plan, including your parents!"

Princess stepped in between the boys. "He's right. Just take it easy."

"I don't need some girl telling me what to do!" Jason screamed.

"Some girl?! You think you're all that because you play FLAG football? I don't know why my grandma thought your dad was such a great kid, because you're a JERK!"

"Hey!" another voice called from the swampy clearing.

"Charlie?" they all said at once. "What are you doing here?"

Charlie, shirtless and still in his football pants, explained, "I got a little freaked out, and I saw y'all head this way."

"Charlie, Aunt Ophelia is going to be freaked out that you're not at the game anymore. She's going to end up in handcuffs next! What were you thinking? And God knows what Grandma will do—she's just crazy enough to end up getting arrested, too!"

"Oh, is she?" the voice of an adult woman pierced the darkness.

"Grandma?" Charlie asked in surprise, running to give her a big sweaty hug.

"Oh, Charlie, eww…so much sweat. Good thing I love your stinky face." She smiled. "You remind me so much of your dad at this age. Princess, what are you doing here?"

"Well, Grandma—" Princess began.

"Oh my goodness!" Nicole Thibodeaux exclaimed. "Are you David Fontenot's son? You have to be—you look just like him. Oh, I loved that kid."

"Seriously, Grandma?" Princess raised her eyebrow. "Was he a jerk, too?"

"Oh, he was a rascal, but a sweet one. How is he?"

"Well, right now, he and my mom are in handcuffs, so I'd say he's been better," snapped Jason.

"I understand that must be upsetting, Jason. I'm so sorry that happened, and it's so unfair. This country was not always like this," Nicole sighed. "What can I do to help?"

And just like that, just as she had won his father's trust so many years ago, Jason immediately trusted Nicole, too, and decided to be nicer to Princess. Princess was intelligent and, he had to admit, very attractive as well, but her lack of awe in his presence annoyed him. The young man was accustomed to always being able to charm others with ease.

"Okay, so, there are some real problems here. I came when I saw Princess AND Charlie were out here."

"Oh, great, now they know where all of us are," Carson sighed.

"Oh, do they?" Nicole smiled as she casually tossed her phone into a nearby waterway. "Here's what I want you kids to do now that I know you're safe. Charlie, first text your mom that you're with me and Princess so she knows you're safe. You two, well—Jason, you stay with us until we know what's going on with your parents. Carson, do your parents know you're safe?"

"Yes, but… there's something important I need to do without them knowing."

"Unfortunately, Carson, I think that will have to wait." Nicole sighed.

Alerts sounded from the remaining phones.

"Weather alert: The storm has increased speed and is predicted to make landfall Tuesday instead of Thursday of next week. Hurricane Camden remains a Category Five hurricane and is expected to be a four or five upon landfall. Evacuation is mandatory."

"Carson, whatever it is needs to wait till after this storm," Nicole said.

"Mrs. Thibodeaux, it cannot wait. It's really important," Jason pleaded.

"Then you can tell me all about it and we'll get it done. Carson, please go home to your parents. I'm sure Jason can handle whatever it is."

"That's the thing. I don't think I can," he said, looking down with embarrassment. "Jason, you remember everything I told you?" Carson asked.

"Wait, what's happening?" Charlie chimed in.

"Long story, cuz," Princess said quietly.

"I remember what you told me," Jason answered.

"I have to evacuate with my family, but here." Carson produced three handheld radio-like devices, complete with extra batteries. "These are vintage things called walkie-talkies that people used to communicate on through radio waves. They aren't even legal, but no one even uses them anymore, so we should have complete privacy. Here's the passcode to make sure we aren't heard."

"Walkie-talkies?" Nicole said. "I haven't seen one of those in years!"

"I read about them once, and I found some in the trash and fixed them up. I thought I'd only need three..." He eyed Charlie and Nicole.

"That's okay, me and Gramma can share," Charlie said.

"Okay, go home now, Carson, and be safe. Now, Jason, since your parents are delayed, I'm taking over caring for you until they can. Not that you can't take care of yourself, but I would feel better knowing I can keep an eye on you—for your dad, okay?"

"Sure." Jason shrugged.

"Alright, first things first, let me see y'all's phones."

"Okay, I guess."

Jason, Charlie, and Princess handed their devices to her without question.

"Oops! Alligators ate our phones," she said as she tossed them into the swampy waterway nearby. The three teens' eyes widened in shock. "Nobody can track us now. Don't worry, Charlie and Princess, I'll get new ones for you, and Jason, I'll make sure you get a new one, too. I promise you, I've been dealing with this horrible government longer than you have. You have no idea what they're capable of, and I will do whatever I can to help. Alaska was the plan, but Mexico may be a better bet. Y'all know Spanish?"

"Look, woman, I'm not going to Mexico with you! My parents are in handcuffs. They're probably gonna get thrown in jail for a day or two, and there's a huge storm coming! I don't know what's wrong with you people. No wonder you didn't say anything about these people, Charlie." Jason snapped, but immediately regretted his emotionally charged reply.

"These people are my family!" Charlie yelled.

"Alright, alright, no one's taking you to Mexico, Jason. I was thinking out loud about myself and my family. Want to come over to make sure Charlie gets home safely?" She winked at Princess.

"You realize I saw you wink?" Jason asked.

"No, you didn't," she laughed and winked again.

"Yep...weird, just like Dad said. I don't know why they liked you so much."

"Hey, now! 'Quirky' is the term I prefer, and we all need to get moving now so nobody tracks us," Nicole said. The teens followed because her presence commanded it.

Upon returning to Charlie's house, there was no sign of his parents, Ophelia and Charlie Senior. Nicole turned to Princess. "Turn that TV on, please."

"Breaking news: more on the riots at Robotics Readiness High tonight. We are here on TunedIN Channel 6 with some of the students and parents who attended the game. Several arrests have been made for disorderly conduct, as well as citations and arrests for violations regarding illegal modes of transportation. The list of those arrested are as follows: David and Jamie Fontenot, with two counts of simple assault of an officer; Ophelia McGinnis for refusing to comply with an officer of the law; and several minors for inciting a riot, assault, and other charges."

"Oh no!" Charlie started to cry.

"It's okay, Charlie. We'll make sure she gets out." Princess hugged her cousin, and Nicole moved to pull both of her grandkids in tightly. Jason stood by awkwardly.

"I'm so sorry about your parents, too, Jason," Nicole said. "I have an idea, though. Can you kids be smart and strong in case I get arrested, too?"

"Wait, what?" Jason asked. "What do you mean 'arrested, too'?"

"I'm gonna break them out." Nicole smiled.

"Whoa, whoa—no offense, but, uh, aren't you kinda old to be doing that kind of thing?" Jason asked.

Nicole laughed. "Age is just a number, dear child."

"Okay, okay...if my dad trusted you, I guess it'll be okay. But you're gonna need Carson. Too bad you sent him away and fed our phones to alligators."

"Oh, I didn't go home." Carson emerged from the other room. "I figured y'all would come here, so I came here instead. I found Mr. Charlie here. He hadn't gotten off work in time to make the game, but he heard on the news Mrs. Ophelia got arrested, and he was very upset and called his lawyer as he headed down to the jail."

"Don't trust your soul to no backwoods Southern lawyer," muttered Nicole.

"What?" Charlie asked, looking confused.

"It's just lyrics to an old song that's since been banned. I'll tell you all about Reba someday, but for now, I'm worried about big Charlie. I just hope he's careful. He and Ophelia can both be so...stubborn sometimes." Nicole sighed.

The teens all remained silent, unsure how to respond.

"Is the jail run by people or robots, or both?" Nicole asked.

"Depends on which one, but seeing as it was a riot, probably the robotic one," Carson responded.

"So we need a very tech-savvy person who's good at finding ways to make things become...delayed."

"A hacker?" Charlie asked.

The others all motioned for him to be quiet; they knew the TV was still on and could record and track potentially threatening conversations.

"How about this? Who can ride horses here?"

They all smiled. They'd all learned this secretly—it was their subtle way of rebelling against an oppressive government that was always tracking them. It was hard to track horses through a swamp, though, and if they ever got caught on foot, they would just plead they had gotten lost.

"So, where are they? You know you'll have to walk, because the cars have tracking devices." Nicole reminded them.

"What if the cars just got unplugged at all the stations with robots?" Jason asked.

"Shhhhh, not so loud," Nicole warned. "I'll take a car, and I have one of the walkies if you need me. Two or three of you just stay together with one. I'll be back soon, hopefully, and if we need to get away if anything goes wrong, just take the horses.

"Carson, if you don't mind, find somewhere safe to buy me some time to free them so they can get away, because they are not spending the storm trapped in a jail cell—that is just not happening. Hack, or do whatever it takes." Nicole left the house and drove off, walkie-talkie hidden under a pile of junk in the front seat of the electric car.

"So, now what?" asked Carson.

"You heard her. Let's go find some horses and get to hackin'," Jason replied. "And Charlie, dude, go put a shirt on, man. You're literally at home—you have clothes here you can change into. You'll want something better than those football cleats to ride in."

"Okay, I'll be right back." Charlie nodded.

"And you! Them Hey Dude things are fun, but you got some real shoes for the swamp?" Jason asked.

"I can use some of Aunt Ophelia's riding boots. We wear the same size. I'll go grab them," Princess agreed. "Good idea, I guess."

"Yeah, not so bad now that your grandma likes me, huh?" Jason asked smugly.

"Dude, just shut up sometimes," Carson said, shaking his head in amusement. "Hey, you got a hacking plan, Mr. Hacker?"

"Yeah, I actually do, but I'll tell you about it when we get there."

CHAPTER 12

UPHEAVAL

The three arrived at the secret barn about twenty minutes later. Princess said quietly, "Come in, Purple Queen, over."

"Purple Queen speaking. Are you at your destination? Over," Nicole responded through the walkie.

"Why is her code name Purple Queen? Like, what does that even mean?" Jason asked Princess as she radioed her grandmother. Princess motioned for Jason to hush.

"Copy that. Arrived safely. Plan in progress. Working on plan to free hostages, over." Nicole replied. "At destination. Your dad already bailed your mom out, Junior, and they are headed home. J, I'm working on it with yours, over."

Carson busily worked on an ancient phone that he had refurbished.

"Okay, I'm in. Give me about ten minutes," he added. "Lights off in ten minutes. Be ready, over."

"Wait, I have an idea," Nicole said. "How secure is this jail during a storm?"

"Uh, it's held up really well for hundreds of years. And it's stocked," Jason said. "Oh, over—do I have to keep saying that?"

"It's fine if you don't. So, it survives storms well?" Nicole responded.

"Yes, pretty well. Why?" Jason replied.

"Please don't turn the lights off yet, C. I'm going to get arrested. We can make a bigger difference inside than out once the storm hits." Nicole's voice came back with her decision.

"Wait! Grandma! NO—what?! It's covered in robotic guards! You'll never get anything done in there," Charlie argued.

"Y'all need to just go back to your aunt's house. I'll be fine. I'm going to hide the walkie outside the jail. I'll escape eventually. Sorry, guys, but please be safe and go home—you're kids. I need to tell the Fontenots that their kiddo is okay, too, so please, just go home. J, you stay at the kids' aunt's house. I'm sure it's fine." Nicole replied.

"Grandma? Grandma? Purple Queen?" Princess spoke into the darkness.

Radio silence echoed through the night.

"Well, we can't just let her do that," Jason sighed. "My parents are in jail...I can't get in trouble too. You two probably should just go back to Charlie's house." He pointed at Princess and Charlie.

"No way!" Charlie exclaimed. "That's my grandma!"

"I'm not going anywhere," Princess said firmly.

"I'm not, either," Carson agreed.

"Y'all know there's a literal hurricane headed this way, and it's beaucoup big?" Jason argued, pointing towards the nearby Gulf.

"Yeah, we know, but we've been through them before," Carson said.

"I have to stay to make sure my parents are okay. I know they don't evacuate jails in time sometimes, especially since they're run by robots and rely on electricity," Jason said with frustration. "The last hurricane, they almost didn't get the prisoners out in time over in a town in Texas because the system shut off due to power outages."

"I know," Princess said solemnly.

"Yeah..." Charlie hung his head.

"What happened?" Carson asked compassionately.

"Our grandpa was one of them. He had a heart attack from all the stress. He had been put in jail for having a rifle his dad passed down to him generations ago that was found buried on their property when they were preparing things for the storm. He wasn't even using it, and he argued with them, but they just put him in jail for both offenses. He had a heart attack on the bus out to the prison, and instead of burying him, they just put him on the side of the road and kept going because they calculated that his burial would have taken time away from getting everyone to safety.

"My grandma saw the whole thing, dragged him home—thankfully he wasn't but half a mile from the jail—buried him, and instead of evacuating, she rode out the storm. She got put in jail for a little while, too, for 'illegally disposing of human remains,' but she never understood how them just leaving him on the road dead wasn't a crime for the robots. She still has nightmares about it."

"Oh my God! That's awful. She's so happy and fun, though...I wouldn't have known," Jason said.

"That's just how she copes with the weight of it all. She feels it deeply, but she goes on for those she loves, especially her kids. She came down here to make sure nothing like that happened to Aunt Ophelia and Uncle Charlie, and I convinced my dad to let me come see my cousins. He didn't want me to, but I begged him, and he's supposed to be coming down to meet us. But with the storm changing direction..." Her voice trailed off.

"No wonder she was willing to get arrested to save people. But I just don't see how she's going to do it from in there," Jason said.

"She talked a lot about her days being a teacher. She truly loved all her students and still does to this day, but she never went back to teaching after that year. I don't know what all happened, but she still won't talk much about it. I know she has bad anxiety, but you'd never know by talking to her because she hides it super well with her friendliness. She went on to be super successful in a different career and owns tons of land in West Texas, but she always felt like teaching was her biggest failure, until what happened with Grandpa Clark. Trying to help your parents is her way of atoning for both my grandpa's death and what she thinks of as a failure many, many years ago, I think."

"Weird …my dad still remembers stuff she taught him. Oh well. I'm glad she succeeded, but dude, she doesn't have to go to jail to save anyone to make up for all that stuff!"

"Princess is right about Grandma. It's why I haven't mentioned her much, or that Mom was her daughter. She wanted it that way. She actually taught my dad, too—that's how Aunt Ophelia met him. They didn't date till years later, but when they did, they hit it off and got married. I hope Mom got all my siblings home safely," Charlie sighed.

"I'm sure they're fine, Charlie," Princess said, patting his head.

"Hey, whoa, you're messing up my vibe, cuz," he laughed.

"What vibe? You're sweaty and stinky and wearing a tank top," Jason teased.

"Hey, it's a shirt! You wanted me to put one on. And it's a muscle shirt, not a tank top," he argued playfully. "Not like you smell like roses, either."

"Okay, the real problem, guys, is that we have no phones, we have a grandma getting arrested, a storm on the way, and no idea if our other plan will even work now," Carson interjected.

"What plan?" Charlie asked.

"Oh, I forgot you didn't know," Jason responded. "Think it's okay to tell him?"

"Yeah, go ahead." Carson nodded.

CHAPTER 13

LAWYERS AND REPORTERS

"See, we had this big plan that was going to take longer, but the storm created the perfect opportunity for us. Do you hate the robotic teachers as much as we do?" Jason asked.

Charlie looked around nervously. One of the horses in the barn whinnied.

"Don't worry, Charlie," Princess assured him. "Grandmas fed our phones to alligators, remember?"

They all laughed a little.

"Also, I don't have parents to worry about," Jason added. "Carson, you do. Princess, you and Charlie do, too. Well, sort of, Princess Peach."

"What did you call me?" Princess protested.

"Princess Peach! Like the old Mario movie." Jason grinned.

"Do NOT call me that." she argued.

"K, Peach." Jason teased.

"Quit flirting, you guys, we've got bigger problems," Charlie said.

"I wasn't—"Jason begin to protest.

"Charlie's right," Carson said. "Let's make a new plan, since Grandma came in and wrecked Plan A, B, and C."

They all laughed a little, but the tension still hung in the air about what to do.

"Okay, so, you were telling me about your plan?" Charlie asked.

"The first one, before alligators and grandmas got involved? What's with you and alligators anyway, Jason?"

"Oh, I gotta hear that story," Princes said with a smile. "But first, let's tell him our plan."

"So, yeah, we hate the robot teachers and want to show the community it's stupid, so we're gonna hack into their system and make it go haywire so we can prove it isn't working. The storm was gonna create the perfect cover for just me and Carson, but then this one overheard us, insisted on being a part of it, and now that I know about her grandpa, I know why, and then you followed us, and then there were alligators, and grandmas, and my parents in jail—"

"Whoa! Like, hack as the kind of hacking that would get you time in federal prison if they catch you?" Charlie's eyes got big.

"Yeah, but we're not gonna get caught. Carson's a genius, and I'm a charmer."

Princess rolled her eyes.

"Oh, come on, you know I'm charming." Jason winked.

To her relief, the darkness covered the shade of red that colored Princess's face. She was too proud to admit she was starting to like this rambunctious fellow, despite his arrogance and quick temper. She saw he truly was a good guy deep down, which was exactly what he tried so hard to hide from the world. She remembered her grandma saying the same about his dad as a young man.

"How about this?" Carson asked. "We all go home, say our phones got smashed in the riot tonight and we got scared, and then we can meet back here tomorrow and plan some more? That way we can all at least get a shower, because I know we stink. No one suspects anything yet, but they'll be putting us up as missing kids soon if we don't turn up, so we should just go home tonight. Plus, then we can find out if your grandma did get arrested."

"Sounds good to me," Jason said. "Can I come home with y'all? My parents are still in jail, as far as I know."

"Sure. You can sleep in my room," Charlie said.

"As long as you shower and wear a dang shirt for a change," Jason joked.

"Hey, my room, my rules! I'll shower, but no promises on the shirt." Charlie joked.

"Okay, let's get back to where we belong, then," Carson said. "Meet here midday tomorrow."

Back at the McGinnis's house, Charlie and Princess explained how they had lost their phones in the chaos and that they thought Grandma had been arrested. "I'll go bail her out immediately," Charlie Senior said.

"Dad, I don't know if she actually was—I just thought she might've been. I saw her with some of the others who got arrested before I ran off," Charlie Junior explained.

"Princess, did you see her?" Aunt Ophelia asked.

"Like Charlie said, I thought she maybe got sent to jail, too."

"Okay, well, I doubt anyone will be open to letting us get you new phones tomorrow, but we can try," Charlie Senior said. "I just don't want y'all to be without a way to talk to us, and I want to be able to track you."

Princess and Charlie looked sheepishly at one another, and then at Jason. "By the way, what's he doing here?" asked Ophelia.

"His parents got arrested. Can he stay here tonight?" Charlie asked.

Ophelia looked at Jason, then at Princess and Charlie.

"Yes, but just know I don't sleep well at night, so I hear EVERYTHING." She eyed Jason suspiciously.

"Yes, ma'am," he said, understanding her implications.

"Geez, Aunt Ophelia! I don't even like him, if that's what you're worried about. He's just a friend of Charlie's."

"Mmm-hmmm, that's what your mom said about me a long time ago." Charlie Senior winked at Ophelia. "She was lying—she's always liked me. She better, since I just bailed her out of jail," he said, kissing her forehead.

"Oh, gross, Mom and Dad, get a room! Like, ew," Charlie Junior protested.

Jason just laughed. "She does like me, she just doesn't want to tell you," he added. "Everyone likes me."

"Oh my goodness, do you *ever* stop talking?" Princess snapped back.

"Alright, clearly I need to go get Grandma out of jail, and Mom needs to stay up all night. I'll be back in a bit," Charlie Senior said, giving Jason a very stern look.

"Let's go get cleaned up, Charlie," Jason said, and the boys headed upstairs.

With that, Charlie Senior headed out to the jail while Ophelia diligently shadowed Princess's every move until she was sure she was asleep. She decided to stay downstairs and watch TV to continue to monitor the situation. She texted Charlie Senior, "Check to see if Fontenots are really in jail. You bonded me out so fast I didn't get a good look. Something suspicious about the kids' behavior tonight. Thanks. Love you. Sorry I got arrested."

Charlie Senior texted back, "Love you too sweetie. I'll check. You and your mom are always causing trouble lol. That's why I love you."

The ancient parish jail was full as Charlie Senior pulled up to scope things out, on the phone with his lawyer again. "Hey, man, I'm sorry to bother you again, but my mother-in-law apparently is in some trouble, too…alright. Thanks. Meet me back at the jail when you can. I am so sorry my family's crazy… yeah. Yeah. The little boys are all home asleep, thankfully. We have David Fontenot's son and my niece over at the house now. I think the Fontenots got busted, too…yeah, I wish I could say what I want to but, you know, always watching. Thanks, man, see you then. I owe you!"

Charlie walked up to the securely guarded jail, and he could hear arguing inside. A news crew from TunedIN was interviewing people outside.

"A football game gone terribly wrong," the peppy reporter, Taylor Trenton, stated. "This is what happens when protests are allowed. There is no such thing as a peaceful protest."

Charlie rolled his eyes, his stomach turning a little at hearing the blatant propaganda that so many people just bought at face value without giving any thought to further consequences.

"We have senior Jessica Valdez here with commentary from the night's events. Jessica, what were you feeling when the riot started?"

Jessica's blonde hair was braided, and she still wore her cheer uniform. "I was, like, 'What in the world?' then I felt terrified. But I was really surprised Mrs. Leichenberg came on the announcements because they seemed pretty mad at her for, like, yelling at kids and stuff."

"Did Mrs. Leichenberg ever yell at you? Do you think that's what started the riots, angry parents?" the reporter asked, pointing the microphone at Jessica.

Jessica, thinking about the potential consequences if Leichenberg was indeed reinstated, just muttered, "No comment."

"What about you, sir? What has your experience been with Mrs. Leichenberg and Robotics Readiness High School?" Taylor asked Mr. Mire who was standing nearby, still worried, as he had not been able to locate Carson yet, despite his phone call.

"I think the idea of the school is wonderful, and I think the future is robotics, but tonight is a prime example of how humans can mess things up badly," he replied thoughtfully, pushing his glasses up slightly as he pondered. "I do think that Mrs. Leichenberg was too harsh, and I am surprised at her reinstatement so quickly after the way she has treated so many students and parents, including myself."

Charlie Senior scanned the crowd, looking for Nicole. No sign of her; however, a bright-red electric car pulled up and Cameron Trahan, the family lawyer, stepped out.

"Cam!" Charlie shouted. "Thank goodness you're here."

Cameron, however, strode straight to the reporter.

"Mr. Trahan, what do you think of tonight's events?" she asked him. "You are a well-respected lawyer in this town. Surely you have some thoughts on how this could have been prevented."

"Actually, I do," Trahan replied, flashing a smile at the cameras. "I believe that we have all forgotten how to be safe in this society. I have been warned that if I continue to help others bond out of jail when they were clearly at fault, I will not be able to continue to practice law. It's a shame my clients cannot see that their actions can only be protected if they line up with the current Constitution, and the new Constitution clearly states that protests of any kind are illegal. I will not be taking any more cases or bonding any more people out of jail. It's too much of a liability, and if you know what's good for you, you'll stop getting arrested."

Charlie Senior's heart sank, but a deep anger rose within him as well.

"How much they pay you to say that, Trahan?" he yelled, storming toward the news crew. "How much?! I thought you had some character still, man! We played ball together. We grew up together. This isn't you!"

"Please step away, Charlie. I cannot help you anymore. You people are going to have to learn how to control yourselves." Trahan began backing away.

"A new and tense situation building at the county jail as Cameron Trahan, a well-respected lawyer, is confronted by Charlie McGinnis Senior, also a local businessman," the news reporter excitedly proclaimed. "Will it escalate further?"

"You people!" Charlie hollered. "What is wrong with this entire country?! You're trying to make things worse, and you just cannot wait to ruin someone's life by blasting them all over the news! My wife just got out of jail for noncompliance with an officer. You know what she did, what was *so* noncompliant? She simply didn't move over fast enough for that infernal robot! I am sick of those machines controlling our lives! And I'm sick of sleazeballs like you, Trahan, only caring about money! You used to help people. That's what you wanted to do, and you helped me earlier, but now, I have lost all respect for you, man. What's the payout for you?"

"Threatening behavior detected in front of the jailhouse," a nearby robotic security officer stated. "Suspect Charlie Robert McGinnis Sr., male, thirty-six years old. Threats to robotic security and to human life-form."

"Oh, but you didn't care about human life-forms when it was my father-in-law lying dead on the ground in that little town in Texas, did you? Then jailing my mother-in-law for burying him when you stupid machines couldn't even figure out that wasn't something you should do! I know the people on the bus tried to help, but you blocked them. You are nothing but a bunch of idiots, and it's so sad my town has come to this. It's about time we just fall into the Gulf, because it would be better to be dead than live like this!"

CHAPTER 14

AN UNEXPECTED ALLY

"Caution: suspect is suicidal. Please escort him to the safe room in the jail until further mental evaluation is available," the robotic security officer stated. "In addition, for the safety of all involved, please return to your homes. Thank you for your service, Miss Trenton. Please be advised the situation has escalated to critical status, and reporting is no longer deemed safe. Please return to the news station and await further instructions."

"Suicidal? *What?* I am *not* suicidal! This is insanity!" Charlie Senior yelled as the robotic guards cuffed him.

Ophelia had been glued to the news, watching the whole thing unfold.

"Mommy?" a little voice said. "Is that Daddy on TV?"

Ophelia quickly turned the TV off. "Oh, Auggie, come here—it will be okay."

Nine-year-old Auggie came and cuddled up to Ophelia. "Is Daddy in jail?"

"Auggie, we are going to figure this out. Please be brave. I know it's scary and we live in a strange world, but I need you to be brave, and please do not tell your little brother. Be strong for him. Is he asleep?"

"Yes, Momma, he's snoring in our room. But what happened to Daddy? Why did they arrest him?"

"How long have you been watching this from behind that door, Auggie?" Ophelia asked. "Since Mr. Trahan turned mean. I don't understand why. He was our friend."

"Oh, baby, sometimes friends turn on us. That is why family is so important. We will always be there for each other."

"What's going on?" Princess asked, appearing in the living room.

"Why are you awake, sweetie?" Ophelia asked.

"Does my dad know not to come? Surely he watched the news and knows it isn't safe. He's never going to let me go anywhere again!" She started crying.

Footsteps on the stairs echoed through the house as Charlie and Jason approached, having heard all the commotion. "What's going on?" Charlie asked.

"Dad got arrested," Auggie said matter-of-factly.

"Auggie!" Ophelia said. "We don't know that yet for a fact. They just took him in to check on him."

"It looked like they arrested him. What does 'suicidal' mean, Mom?" Auggie asked.

Ophelia's heart filled with heaviness and sadness. This was not the world she had imagined for her children.

"Hey, little bud, it'll be okay. Your dad is smart, and he knows the right people," Jason said.

"Oh, Jason, the right people have been bribed, unfortunately." Ophelia sighed.

"What? Trahan? I knew he was a sleazeball from the time I met his kid. No one believed me, though. That kid is the one who ratted me out for the alligator." Jason recalled.

"What alligator?" Princess asked.

"Well, we could probably all use a laugh, huh?" Ophelia said. "Why don't you tell us the alligator story, Jason?"

"I love this story," Auggie piped up. "I'm gonna bring alligators to school someday!"

"Dude, let him talk," Charlie reprimanded his brother.

"Alright, y'all ready for this?" His chest puffing up, Jason proceeded to tell the events leading up to the alligator prank that had almost landed him in jail and caused him to have several days of suspension. "It was just a little one. Like this big." He motioned a length of about three feet with his hands.

"More like *this* big." Charlie grabbed his hands and pulled them to about five feet apart.

"Bruh, you weren't even in high school yet. How do *you* know?" Jason chuckled.

"I saw the pictures on TunedIN and the news! Plus, everyone had it all over their social media accounts until they got fined for talking about it."

"I still have a picture of it anyway," Jason grinned.

Princess shook her head. Ophelia giggled because she did not know what else to do, which caused a ripple effect of laughter, and it eased the night's tension somewhat. After the laughter subsided, though, she stated solemnly, "We have a real issue. We don't know who we can trust, your dad is in jail, we still don't know if he found Grandma, your parents are possibly still in jail, Jason, and—"

"Mommy?" a sleepy little brown-haired boy wandered out of his room. "I heard a lot of noise."

"Oliver, sweetie, it's all okay. You can go back to sleep." Ophelia assured her youngest son.

Charlie grabbed the remote and turned the TV back on, "I want to know what happened to Dad, Mom. Just go back to bed, Ollie," Charlie pleaded.

"Wait, look!" Princess pointed to the TV.

"Breaking news from the Channel Six News Station. Due to rising tensions in the area, the uncertainty of the upcoming storm, and the potential for more riots if left unchecked, all citizens are required to begin mandatory evacuations starting tonight. Anyone who has not left by noon tomorrow will be relocated for their own safety. We will escort the prisoners after the remaining population has been relocated. The relocation center is in Southeast Arkansas, safe in the mountains.

"Anyone who attempts to stay will be fined and considered in contempt of court upon return if they are found alive. However, the likelihood of surviving a Category Four or Five storm is minimal, which is why it is imperative to follow evacuation orders. In order to conserve electricity, please avoid using your cars tonight and ensure they have a full charge. If you do not have transportation, the local electric buses have been preparing for the evacuation. You must have a cellular device to ride, and if you do not, you will be provided with one that will be taken out of your earnings after the storm. Tracking everyone is imperative during a time of emergency. Thank you for your cooperation."

"Oh, boy," Ophelia said. "New plan: We get to that jail, we make sure everyone is okay, and we hijack that bus that will be taking everyone out. We'll make sure the people who want to stay here will be on that bus so we can find a way to defend our home while the robots are out of commission. I don't exactly know how, but kids, do you trust me?"

"I'm scared, Mommy," seven-year-old Oliver said.

"It's okay, Oliver. I am, too, but you can be brave like me," Auggie encouraged.

"So, the new plan is what?" Jason asked.

"Everyone just grab a few changes of clothes, grab some toilet paper and water bottles, and get in the car. Charlie, grab our tents and camping stuff and batteries and flashlights. I need everyone to be brave and trust me. We are all going to be together soon, and we are going to fix this world for you kids, or at least die trying. For my dad, who died needlessly, we have to go help those people," Ophelia said.

After rushing to gather their supplies, the family piled into the small electric car and headed down to the jail.

"I need you kids to walk in with me calmly," she said. "No outbursts, okay?" She eyed Jason.

"Geez, why you looking at me?" he asked.

"Oh, I don't know, maybe because you're a hothead who goes around throwing his helmet, charging at robots. Something along those lines," Ophelia snapped back.

"Fair enough. Okay, I'll keep it cool."

Jason nodded in agreement.

"Please, for my family's sake, you've got to. Please, Jason." Princess looked at him with imploring eyes, and Jason felt the need to protect her and her family at all costs. He knew that he struggled with his temper, but he also knew he had a way with words and charm that would benefit them all.

Although they were all tired, as it was now around three a.m. on Saturday morning, the adrenaline kept them going. They all had at least gotten a little nap, and now they were ready to take on the next challenge, whatever that may be.

The family entered the jail calmly and quietly, requesting to speak to their loved ones. "You are permitted to see your mother and father, Jason. You will be escorted by Officer Antonio Moreno," one of the guards said.

To Jason's surprise, Moreno was human. "Mrs. McGinnis, you and the boys will go down that hall." The guard pointed to a long hall across the jail and the McGinnis family, along with Princess, followed another robotic guard with hopes of seeing their father and uncle.

"I thought this was mainly a robotics jail?" Jason asked Officer Moreno.

"Well, they're sending out most of them to protect them from the storm, but they're a little behind schedule. The ones that may end up left behind have secure containers they'll be stored in nearby," Moreno explained.

"Classified information is not permitted to be given to outsiders," a security robot droned as it passed by.

"Kid, I hated seeing your parents get locked up. I'm doing my best to make a difference here, but my hands are kind of tied," Moreno whispered. "But I'm going to have an emergency in a minute here you need to be on the lookout for." His eyes spoke more than his words did.

"Come this way, I'll let you in." Moreno pulled his keys off his security belt and unlocked the door. "Oh, no, I hear a security breach in another part of the building! Is your software malfunctioning, Officer Finn?"

"Software is up-to-date and functioning," Finn replied. "Please secure the cell door, Officer Moreno."

"I think you are malfunctioning, sir," Moreno said. "I heard a noise." He eyed the Fontenots with body language that said *Keep your mouth shut, but trust me.*

"Malfunction not detected," Officer Fin replied. Suddenly, a loud bang of thunder crashed through the sky, and the lights flickered. Almost as if it had been orchestrated with incredibly precise timing, all of the robotics shut down after a few loud beeps.

In the next cell, Leichenberg could be heard snoring loudly, her breath heavy with the scent of alcohol.

"Jason! Thank God you're okay!" Jamie ran to her son and hugged him through the cold, steely bars. "I don't think she actually got reinstated," Jamie whispered to Jason, pointing to Leichenberg. "I think she slipped past security and made that announcement to make sure to punish the parents and students she blames for her failures. What better way than to incite a riot? She'll probably be charged for it."

The lights flickered again and loud beeps echoed through the old jailhouse, this time awakening Leichenberg. And it was no calm awakening, as she woke up cursing and shouting about how she'd been promised that job and the robots stole her job because of horrible parents and kids.

"Like you!" She spotted Jamie Fontenot in the other cell. "Your horrible kid is the one that started all this!"

"You better be glad there's bars between us, or you'd be learning a lesson you won't soon forget," Jamie snapped.

"Guard, she's threatening me. I want a human guard! Moreno, you'll pay for this!" Leichenberg slurred.

"Your money isn't gonna save you anymore. We found out why you got sent away from the other schools, and it had nothing to do with robots. I'm not a bit surprised you're drunk as a skunk, and I hope you know tonight's chaos is your fault," Moreno shot back.

"That's right, you foul woman," David Fontenot added with a glare.

"I'm going to step away and check on the rest of the prisoners, alright?" Moreno nodded toward the keys in the door. "I know we need to get everyone to a bus or a boat that's down at the beach."

The Fontenots picked up on the unspoken clues Moreno was leaving them.

"Hey, Mom, Dad, have you seen a lady named Nicole in here?" Jason asked.

"Nicole? Nicole who?" asked David.

"She's old—Nicole Thibodeaux. She said she was your teacher many years ago."

"Mrs. Thibodeaux got arrested?" David asked, then laughed. "Of course she did. She never knew how to keep her mouth shut, but she was fun. But I haven't seen her. What's going on with Charlie Senior, though? I saw them dragging him into the mental health holding ward!"

"Oh, they took something he said and twisted it. And we got a rat. Trahan is a huge rat, and he's getting paid off to please the robotic government people. He was helping Charlie Senior, but then they got to him. That's what set off Big Charlie. Little Charlie is fine, and his cousin is, too." Jason explained.

"Cousin?" David looked confused

"I'll explain later. We gotta find Mrs. Thibodeaux if she's here," Jason urged.

"I'm here, alright," they heard a voice from the end of the hall.

"Thibodeaux? What a nightmare!" Leichenberg shouted. "My cousin told me about you and your stupid ideas. You made her life HELL!"

"She made *my* life hell!" Thibodeaux hollered back. "Sounds like the apple doesn't fall too far from the tree, because you seem like a horrible person, too! I have found my voice, and you will not bully me like she did so mercilessly back in our high school days and even on to our career days!"

"Wait? You know each other?" David Fontenot asked.

"Of each other—long story. I was willing to give this one a chance, but she's worse than the original," Thibodeaux said. "Also, I can barely breathe—you reek of cheap cigarettes."

"Maria said you always were a goody two-shoes who didn't know how to do normal stuff. Why don't you just accept that we're in the same boat and have some wine?" Leichenberg pulled out a bottle of wine that had been hidden in her jacket.

"Oh, man, I wish I had my phone," Jason said.

"Here, take mine," Jamie offered. "We'll make sure she doesn't get to bully anyone ever again."

"Turn that off right now! This is nonsense!" Leichenberg continued to shriek and yell.

"Okay, if you can hear yourself think over that, let's get out of here," Jason said, using the keys that Moreno had so conveniently forgotten only to discover they had a small map attached. "I'll let Thibodeaux out, but what do we do with her?" he pointed to Leichenberg.

"How about we come back when she's sober?" Thibodeaux suggested.

"Or just leave her to rot," Jason snapped.

"No, we cannot do that. Her life is still valuable, and I cannot let those machines turn me into one of them as well. Horrible as she seems, she's still human." Nicole sighed.

"I can hear you! You all will be so–so–rryyyyy!" Leichenberg slurred her speech and fell backwards onto the cot, passing out again, only to revive for a minute. The kid in the cell beside her asked for a drink of her wine, and she passed it to them willingly.

The Fontenots and Thibodeauxs shook their heads. "JoJo, I know you're stressed, but you gotta be alert, man. Give that back to her," Jason pleaded. "I'll get you out, man."

Leichenberg had passed back out, and JoJo complied.

"Who all else is here?" Jason asked him.

"Blaize, Dante, and Talia all are here somewhere. I don't know where they took Coach. I think the girls are in the next cell block, but there are still guards that are functional, so we'll have to wait for more lightning."

The sun was beginning to rise as the long night gave way to daylight. The nearby waves could be heard crashing on the shores of the Gulf of Mexico. The saltwater air wafted through the town, with ominous clouds creeping in behind.

"Where's Mrs. Ophelia?" asked Jason as he and his parents along with Nicole, Blaize, Dante, and Talia navigated the jail, careful not to be seen. '

They planned their moves carefully in time with the thunder and lightning and light flickers.

In one moment when the lights came back on briefly, though, much to their surprise, not a single robot was moving. It was as if they had been disabled.

Jason smiled. Carson had done it—but it was early to be celebrating. He also couldn't let on that he knew; there were too many people who needed protection from implication in the plan.

Jason also knew that after tonight, nothing about his life would go back to normal. The likelihood of a normal senior year had evaporated with the riot at the football game, but the breakdown had been happening from the very beginning.

"Hey! Over here!" the group heard a voice coming from down the hall.

"Do you have keys?" Ophelia asked.

"Sure do," David replied. "Is big Charlie okay?"

"Yes, and he isn't suicidal, they just twisted his words so they could lock him up. But be careful—Trahan's going to catch wind of this soon if we don't act fast. Did you know this building has a lower floor?" Ophelia asked.

"There's a hurricane that's gonna hit in two days now; it's sped up. That lower level is gonna be full of water," David reminded her.

"Oh, just for tonight. It has restrooms, a shower, and some cots from a long time ago. We can at least get some rest until we decide what to do further."

"Great idea," Jamie said.

"Hey, I know there's a lot of other stuff down there they've offered to us coaches in the past," Coach Hoffner said as he walked up.

"How did you get out?" Jamie asked.

Coach Hoffner just shrugged. "Man's got his ways," he said. "And JoJo, don't let me *evah* catch you taking no alcohol from nobody, 'specially not that witchy woman."

"Yes, Coach." JoJo hung his head. "I was just really stressed."

"It's okay, boy. Just that I know you're better than that, and you ain't old enough anyway."

"Alcohol can really screw up your brain if you're young, and it can tear families apart if someone gets addicted," Ophelia explained.

Tears started to fall from Nicole's eyes as she put her arm around her daughter. They exchanged an unspoken look that spoke volumes; they each remembered the days over forty years ago when alcohol had almost ruined their family, but it was the distant past. "It's okay. I'll be okay, sweetie. I'm just tired. She's right—some people can handle it, some cannot. But you never know till you take the first sip, and if you cannot, then the first sip can ruin your life." Everyone fell silent until Coach Hoffner spoke again, taking charge of the situation.

"Okay, well, let's all head down to the basement. There's some MREs down there, and maybe even some old juice and chips. Nobody goes down there anymore. We'll keep an eye on the time; I grabbed an old watch from one of the drawers here. That way, we'll know when we have to come up to get out away from the storm. Hiding out is the best option right now."

"Wait!" a voice called out.

"Carson?" Jason looked surprised.

"I think they figured it out, but they don't know it was me yet. They're searching my parents' house. It was happening when I got home—they went ahead and evacuated them and are hunting for me. Is the lower level safe for me, too? I think I can fix it to get them off our trail." Carson said.

"Yeah, let's head down right now." Jason agreed.

"Did Leichenberg hear any of this, though? We can't just leave her up there to blab," Jamie pointed out.

"What do you suggest we do with her, then? I don't want to be stuck in a basement with that woman!" Ophelia protested.

"She's so drunk, I doubt she'll remember anything, and it's just a chance we'll have to take. We'll get to her after we come back up. Someone help me grab one of these robots that's dead." Charlie Senior suggested.

"Why?" asked Ophelia.

"So we'll know when it comes back on and what to expect. We can handcuff it to something down there. Go grab some cuffs from that drawer." Charlie Senior explained.

Moreno appeared again and nodded his approval of the plan. "I'll say the robots malfunctioned and let you all out before I could catch any of you. Someone shut me in a cell—you can come back for me later."

"You sure?" Charlie Senior looked concerned

"Yeah, I think it helps cover for y'all best. Boys, y'all be quiet down there, understand?" Moreno warned the younger boys, hoping they'd grasp the seriousness of the situation.

"Yes, sir," the little boys agreed.

"Big boys, too, and girls. Not a sound for the next couple hours! Go take a bathroom break, and for the love of God, get some sleep. We're all gonna need it."

CHAPTER 15

DECISIONS

The robotic security guard sat upright in a corner, both hands hand-cuffed to a stair railing leading up to the top floor. It wasn't a basement so much as a bottom floor to a building on stilts, but it still provided the necessary means of hiding that was essential for the group of people it offered shelter.

"I hope my parents are okay," Carson lamented. "I just got scared and ran... I heard they were bringing them up to the Arkansas evacuation center for questioning. I just hope the storm destroys the evidence, because I was able to disable the robotic guards searching my house before I got away. They should come out clean, but I don't know what will happen to them, or to me. I don't want to go to federal prison! I heard it's nothing like it once was."

"It'll be okay, Carson. I think we all are in danger of that right now after tonight." Nicole sighed. "But for now, it's almost dawn, and none of us have slept yet. We need to be quiet for a while anyway."

"She's right, boys. Help me get those cots over there." Coach Hoffner pointed to the dusty stack of cots. "We all need to rest before the next step."

"Daddy, what if we're stuck here in the storm?" Ollie asked. "I'm scared!"

"Ollie, we won't be. We'll make sure you are protected," Charlie

Senior reassured his youngest son, patting his head. "Go to your cot and go to sleep, son."

As dawn broke, the weary group finally rested, unaware of what was happening above them but hoping they would remain undiscovered.

By about three the next afternoon, everyone on the lower floor had awakened.

"I wish we had a way to find out if it's safe to go up there," Ophelia said as she gently rocked a still very sleepy Auggie. "It's time to get up and find some food, though."

"They got a whole buncha snacks over there," Coach Hoffner said. "They may be expired, but they're still food."

"Oh, yeah! Takis!" Charlie Junior said excitedly.

"Please no!" Blaize said.

"Yeah, uh, let's eat something that's gonna be less stinky later, since we're all in such close quarters," Charlie Senior laughed.

"Shhh, do you hear that?" David Fontenot motioned for them to be quiet. "Where are our kids?" a woman's voice yelled. "Dante?" Dante's mother's voice echoed down to the lower floor. "Dante? Blaize... JoJo?"

"Hey, over here!" they heard Moreno say. "The kids are down-stairs, but don't say anything about me telling you. You can take them home, just be careful. I don't know what all is going on out there after last night," Moreno explained.

"You want us to let you out? What happened?" Amos, Dante's father, asked. "It's chaos out there. I don't even know if we're going to make the bus for the evacuation, but we need to, because Dante's gotta have his medication. He's got asthma, and we can't be without power. We can't really do much because we have to help him, but if we don't listen to them, they'll withhold his medicine—he almost died last time he had an asthma attack after we ran out of his medication because we couldn't afford to pay the fine I got for growing some tomatoes."

Leichenberg had awakened and was incredibly hungover in the next cell, rubbing her pounding head. "Can you let me out, too, so I can catch that bus?"

The parents eyed each other.

"We should let your sorry self rot here," Dante's mother, Jayla, spat. "Especially after you letting them robots teach them such nonsense, like that racism isn't real when it happens to more than just Black folks. Look at what they've done to the Jewish people here in America! And some of the Chinese Americans were definitely victims of racism after the second wave hit—we just aren't supposed to talk about it because the new Constitution says so, but I'm tired of it. I'm tired of being silenced."

"Right?" replied Talia's mother, Hadassah. "You know good and well there are people who would send me straight back to the Middle East if they found out I was Jewish. The community protects me, and we've changed our last name, but it's been harder and harder to hide with the intense hatred that's been going on ever since the Third World War broke out. Just a few hours away in New Orleans last week, they sent another Jewish family back to Israel, if that's even where they actually sent them. They were completely legal Americans, the third or fourth generation here, who had escaped Germany right before World War II. Sadly, ironic, isn't it? Yet we aren't allowed to say a word; I'm free to speak now only because these machines seem to have miraculously malfunctioned long enough for me to say anything."

Leichenberg stared aimlessly. She sighed.

"Hey!" a voice called from downstairs. "Let her out."

"Who are you?" asked Jayla.

"My name is Nicole. I don't know what made her the way she is, but she doesn't deserve to die in a hurricane in a jail cell. They won't even bother to bury her."

"Well, deserve it, she may, but that's beside the point," Hadassah agreed. "We cannot stoop to the level of our enemies. If we don't unite, we will continue to see horrors like we've already seen."

The rest of the children and adults from downstairs followed behind Nicole, wondering what would happen next.

"Exactly," Moreno agreed. "Let her out. I'll stay behind and take care of anyone who feels like they would end up in jail if they evacuated, and the rest of you get to that bus. Someone let the horses out so they have a chance of survival, too, but save us a few in case we need them. We'll make sure they're looked after."

Moreno's voice was gentle but commanded obedience. His tough Italian exterior often made others fear him, but he was indeed a very conscientious man. He hated the government takeover, and he had been fighting it quietly as best he could. His brawny arms boasted a faded "Semper Fi" tattoo, a faint reminder of the once-great country he had put his life on the line for over thirty years before, before America had become what it now was.

He had connections in Texas, and there was talk of lands in Mexico that were still untouched. Even the Chinese and American governments were afraid to go near those desolate places, as they were deemed very dangerous—and rightfully so, in some instances. Moreno's plan was to get as many people as he could down to Mexico with him. He had not anticipated it being this soon, but nothing about anyone's plans seemed to be unfolding as they thought lately.

One of the shorted security robots made a slight movement that made some of the parents gasp, but thunder crashed and the robot fell to the floor.

"Alright, who's staying and who's going?" Moreno asked. "We need to act fast."

Hadassah spoke up, "JoJo, Blaize, I know your parents were looking for you, but they were headed this way and were delayed by the traffic piling up. Everyone's panicking because the electric cars didn't all charge overnight, and so they're having to pull out the generators at city hall to charge the big buses to evacuate everyone. The robotic drivers all shut down—it's just a nightmare. We also heard on TunedIN that the president was sending some of those really powerful robotic soldiers to put a stop to this chaos, so we need to act fast. However, I'm sending you two with Dante's parents.

"Talia and I are going to stay behind. We're headed home to take our chances there. I'd rather die in a hurricane than be subjected to what may await us elsewhere. It's already dangerous enough being Jewish, but our presence is going to make it more dangerous for anyone we go with, so we will go home to my husband and pray for the best. Is it okay if they head out with y'all?" she asked Dante's parents.

Dante's parents agreed, and Blaize and JoJo complied. The kids all hugged each other and held back tears, because they knew it was quite possibly the last time they would see one another.

"Carson, I heard your parents safely arrived on the first stop on the bus to Arkansas, but they're still being questioned. But because they were on some safe parents list, they think maybe someone framed them," Jayla added. "I just thought you'd wanna know. You coming with us, too?"

"No, ma'am," Carson sighed. "It was me. I'm the one who caused the malfunctions, but I'm glad my parents aren't in trouble. Tell them I'm okay if you can, but don't let anyone know you know anything, please. For your safety and theirs."

"Oh, honey," Jayla sighed. "I know...I know. It's a sad and scary place to live, but I know. They watch us like hawks."

"Anyone still have a cell phone that could have been recording?" asked Moreno.

"We have ours on incognito for now," Amos replied. "No worries, the storm probably's jamming the signal anyway if even those robots are dead; my phone shouldn't be a problem."

"And ours got eaten," muttered Jason.

"What?" asked Jamie Fontenot.

"Nothing." He shrugged. "Just lost my phone, that's it."

"Hey, uh, can someone please let me out?" Leichenberg asked, still rubbing her head.

"Here's the deal," David Fontenot said. "I'll let you out, but if you as much as breathe a word of our plan, I'll know. I'll know, and I'll post that video of you offering a minor wine all over TunedIN before they drag my butt to jail for my 'plot.' Are we clear? I'll send this phone with Jayla, and she will do it with no hesitation. Do you understand?"

Leichenberg shook her head, too tired to argue or even be angry. She took one last swig of her hidden bottle of wine.

The rest of them exchanged looks with a mix of pity and anger.

"I hope you find some peace," Nicole said.

Leichenberg, the Dante, Blaize, and JoJo left with Jayla and Amos, and Hadassah and Talia headed home as well. No sooner had they left, another figure came rushing into the jailhouse.

CHAPTER 16

STRANGE SHELTER

"D ad!" Princess screamed. "Mom!"

"Oh, thank God you're okay!" Kallie Thibodeaux exclaimed.

"Micah!" Nicole cried and ran to embrace her son.

"How did you make it past all the chaos?" Ophelia asked.

"Uncle Micah!" Auggie and Ollie exclaimed as they came running around the corner.

"Hey guys!" he said, picking up his nephews. "We came when we saw the riot. We figured Mom would get in trouble."

"Well, thanks a lot, son," Nicole laughed.

"She's not wrong," Ophelia agreed.

"Says the woman who *also* got in trouble," Charlie Senior teased.

"Hey, we're all in the same boat now," David Fontenot chimed in, but was drowned out by another loud clap of thunder. "Alright, what's the plan, Moreno?"

"Well, you've heard how Mexico has some land that's still decently uninhabited, but you can farm it?" Moreno asked.

"Yes, and in fact, we have quite a large lot of land in Del City that's on the border, and a whole underground bunker full of supplies if we can get there," Nicole answered.

"No need. I have friends in Mexico who have a stocked piece of land, with enough supplies for at least thirty people for as long as it takes to get a self-sustainable homestead going. It's far enough out that the satellites have trouble picking up on what's going on, and while it's dangerous because it isn't far from the area where the cartel runs their drugs, it's also safe for that same reason. Even the Chinese don't want to mess with the Mexican drug lords. My friends down there are Mexican Americans who returned to Mexico right before the second pandemic because they were afraid of what would happen to this country. The trick, of course, will be getting past the border."

"Unless we took a boat," Coach Hoffner suggested.

"In the middle of a hurricane?" Jason interjected, raising an eyebrow.

"After the hurricane, not during it," Hoffner said. "I used to run a shrimp boat with my dad."

"Who knows how and where we'd find a boat big enough for all of us, and where are we going to ride out this storm where the soldiers won't find us?" Charlie Junior asked.

"I have a boat ready, actually," Moreno said. "I've had one ready for a long time, but it's gonna have to wait till after the storm, and we're gonna have to hope that it survives the storm in the first place. If not, we'll have to find another one.

"Also, yes, it's a long trip to Mexico, but the boat would be a better idea. The border guards are not going to let us through, and they've got all kinds of new traps to keep us from escaping to Mexico; I think they think of new ways to kill people daily. For now, though, we have to stay alive because a literal hurricane is headed this way, and we have no way to know if it's worse or better than we think because we cannot risk being tracked."

"I have an idea!" Charlie Senior said. "Let's go to the school! No one will think to look for us there, and we'll have all we need if we can get there fast. It's already almost nightfall, it's raining, and the power is going in and out. We'll just be really quiet and watch the security cameras to see if someone's coming!"

Nicole's face filled with dread. "Do we have to?"

"Come on, Mom, it's going to save us," Micah explained. "If you can bury Dad and survive all that, you can go back in that building."

"I know, I know…I'm sorry. It is the best solution. Let's do it."

"Maybe we'll find you some cheese," David quipped.

Nicole gave him one of her famous teacher looks, and for a moment, time stood still.

"Oh, here comes the teacher look!" laughed Charlie Senior. "Come on, let's go, we gotta move! We still need to let out the horses, or bring them to the school."

"Horses at school?" Ollie laughed. "That's funny!"

They were able to ensure the horses were safe in the school's long-forgotten agriculture barn before heading for the front doors of the school.

At Robotics Readiness High, there was an eerie quietness that hung in the air as its temporary inhabitants entered the building. Officer Moreno had a key to the school and knew the security system passcode, while Carson was able to ensure no one was tracking them by utilizing his brilliant skills to override anything that may have caused suspicion.

"We have to be quick and quiet, because movement and lights are going to alert the soldiers when they get here. I think the gym is the best place to be once we get everything situated. It's the safest, too, for the storm that's going to hit tomorrow," Coach Hoffner explained. "The locker rooms are probably the safest inside the gym because there aren't any windows, and after every storm, the locker room was always the least touched place. Plus, we got snacks and extra clothes in there. If y'all want some hoodies, kids, grab them from the extra room down that hall.

"Jason, Charlie, go to the cafeteria and gather all the canned food you can find and cart it down here to the locker rooms. Princess, you and your brothers gather the deodorant from the supplies room—they can show you where—because we don't need any stinky kids. Everyone is gonna shower before this storm comes, too, because we gonna be sweating like crazy once the power really goes out.

"Big Charlie, you, David, and me are gonna set up pallets for the kids in the women's locker room. We'll let the men and women take turns in the showers and then we can settle in for the night. We all probably wanna be in the same room, because them kids are gonna be scared."

"Sounds good," Moreno said. "I'll go sit and watch the security cameras. I wish we had a way to communicate where no one could track us, though."

"Like this?" Nicole asked, producing her walkie-talkie. "Kids, y'all still have yours?"

Jason and Princess pulled theirs out.

"I don't wanna know how you got those," Moreno chuckled. "But perfect. Nicole, wanna come watch the cameras with me?"

"Sure, why not? It'll be interesting to be the one watching for once instead of being watched," she laughed.

"They'll work till the power goes out. That's the only thing—once the power goes out, we have to head back to the gym. Hoffner, you got flashlights?"

"Yep, right here. Lotsa batteries, too. We should be good." Coach Hoffner replied.

Nicole and Moreno headed down the dark hall to the front office, and Nicole's emotions raged as they walked into the long-forgotten place. She eyed the spot on the floor where she'd once tripped and spilled her water all over the carpet; she shuddered as she thought of the reaction she'd had.

She had been young and naive, believing the world to be mostly good. That simple spill had been a foreshadowing of things to come. Nicole's entire life would soon spill on the floor as she tried and tried to clean it up without causing more damage. However, full cups overflow, both physically and metaphorically, and that had happened to her so long ago. She had learned since then not to carry full cups without tightly sealed lids, and not to let them overflow.

"You okay?" Moreno asked, seeing her expression.

"Oh—yeah. I used to work here a very long time ago." Nicole said quietly.

"Oh, really? I didn't know that. Bet they'd be glad to know you were back." Moreno observed.

"No, they wouldn't. Well, some would, but...it's a long story. I was young and naïve, and if you've ever seen the movie *The Sound of Music*—I mean, I doubt it, because it's banned—but if you had—" Nicole's voice trailed off; there were so many things they had lost that were beautiful works of art, no longer legal.

"I have." Moreno smiled. "I remember watching it as a kid with my mom."

"Before the war?" Nicole asked.

"Yes. Let me guess, you were like solving a problem like Maria?" Moreno chuckled.

"Something like that." Nicole laughed.

Moreno grinned. "I thought as much. If you don't mind my asking, where's the husband?"

Nicole's dark eyes brimmed with tears.

"Oh, I'm sorry... I–I didn't know." Moreno stammered. "I was just trying to make conversation since we're gonna be stuck here awhile."

"It's okay. It's just painful to talk about." She wiped away the tear that had escaped her eyes.

"Hey, Mrs. T!" David Fontenot popped in about that time. "I got you some water."

"Thanks, sweetie," Nicole said as she halfheartedly reached for it, and it spilled a little as David handed it to her. "Dang it, David! Still?! You're a grown man now. Seriously?" she laughed.

"That was a much needed diversion, though."

"You making her cry?" David asked, glancing over at Moreno

"No, no, David, nothing like that. He didn't know about what happened to my husband."

"Mr. Clark? That legend?" David asked.

"Yeah, well, it's not so legendary what happened to him. It's part of why I'm here helping with this plot to take down some of these ridiculous machines. I just don't want to talk about what happened quite yet," Nicole said quietly.

"Okay, okay. That's fine. I just wanted to make sure y'all were okay. Be good to her, 'k?" David eyed Moreno.

"I'm fine, David. Go take care of Jamie and the kids. I'm capable of handling myself. Remember my story about when I visited Argentina?" Nicole asked.

"You're lucky you didn't get kidnapped, but yeah. Maybe I should tell you to be careful, Moreno." David grinned.

"Oh, I'm capable of handling anything!" Moreno smiled. "I was a Marine, back when that meant something."

"Dad? What are *you* doing in here?" Jason entered the office next.

"What are *you* doing in here?" Princess asked, appearing behind Jason.

"What is everyone doing in here?" asked Charlie Junior, coming in behind them.

"Okay, guys, I'm perfectly fine! Officer Moreno doesn't need help. Go back and do whatever Coach needs you to do," Nicole answered them, laughing.

"Yes, ma'am," David said. "Y'all heard her, get!"

"You, too, David," she added.

"Alright, alright." David headed back to his designated area with the kids in tow.

"Wait! Did you see that?!" Nicole asked, pointing to the screen.

"Yes I did," Moreno answered solemnly, picking up the walkie-talkie. "Come in, all channels. Go immediately to the locker rooms and do NOT make any noise. The robotic soldiers have arrived. I will try to make out what they're saying, but the audio isn't good. Sounds like they're looking for us. We are determined to be missing and 'wanted.' Apparently, the story is that you kidnapped me. I repeat, go to the locker rooms and do NOT make a sound. Nicole and I are going to stay in here and keep watch."

He turned to Nicole. "That means we need to hide, though. Good thing this desk is huge. Who needs this big of a dang desk?" he laughed, motioning for her to come under the desk with him.

CHAPTER 17

PAINS OF THE PAST

"Really?" Nicole whispered, raising her eyebrows at the idea of hiding under the imposing desk.

"You want to get caught by robotic soldiers?" asked Moreno

"Fine, I'm coming," she agreed, scooching under the desk beside him.

"We can still see the cameras from here," he whispered, then spoke into the walkie-talkie, "Thankfully, they're nowhere near the school yet. I don't think they'll suspect this is where we went; they're searching our homes first. One good thing about robots is they cannot predict human unpredictability yet. Oh, and one more thing—until I give the all clear, no more radio communication." He clicked the walkie-talkie off.

"Hey," Nicole said softly. "Do you have a family that'll be worried about you?"

Toni Moreno rarely showed his vulnerable side, but it was evident his emotions were high as he considered her question.

"I'm sorry," she quickly responded. "I didn't mean to upset you. I'll tell you what happened to my husband."

He motioned for her to hush as he pointed at the screens. The robots were now passing the school. One eyed the keypad at the entrance and droned, "Entry detected approximately two hours ago."

"Building is secure, locked, and appears empty," noted another bot.

Carson had thankfully remembered to program the system to appear as if security had checked the building at the precise time they had entered.

"Standard security procedure recorded at eight forty-nine p.m. Nothing unusual noted."

"All robotic instructors have been removed from the building and relocated to an undisclosed safe location. Two robotic medics were left behind in case of emergency."

"Hurricane strength has dropped to a Category Four. This storm remains dangerous for human life and artificial-intelligence agents. All artificial-intelligence agents, please report back to the evacuation bus. The search for the escaped fugitives will continue after the storm. Likelihood of survival in the elements is a one-in-one-hundred chance. If not found within seventy-two hours after the storm, all fugitives will be presumed dead."

"A jolly bunch of fellows, aren't they?" Moreno whispered.

Nicole stifled laughter with her hands as her body shook. The tension had been so great that the much-needed laugh rocked her entire body.

"Are you crying?" Moreno mouthed.

She signaled to him that she was laughing, and then he couldn't help but laugh a bit, too, making her motion for him to hush, which just made them both have to hold back their laughter more.

They ended up back-to-back, shaking in the laughter they were desperately trying to hold back. The laughter soon turned to tears for Nicole. Moreno wasn't sure what to do, so he put his arm around her and just let her cry into his chest. They both had endured so much pain throughout the past twenty years, and they didn't even have to speak to understand that they both had endured something tragic.

For a few moments, humanity reigned supreme as two broken-hearted humans embraced under a bulky desk that had once been a source of fear for Nicole. The desk was nothing now, though, compared to what she'd been through seeing her husband left dead in the street, discarded like trash.

After about thirty minutes that seemed like an eternity, Moreno pulled away and picked up the walkie-talkie. "All clear. I believe we're safe. Stay where you are—we will come to you. Y'all okay?"

"Yes, we're fine. The little guys are already asleep," Coach Hoffner answered. "If you want showers, I'd head over now and you can take turns. I'll stand guard outside so nobody bothers you. We're gonna take the next thirty minutes to get that out of the way, then it's bedtime for all of us. We got a long night ahead. I hear the winds howling outside already."

"Sounds good. We'll be down shortly." Toni turned to Nicole. "You okay?"

"Yes. I'll tell you a little bit on the way. Thanks…sorry I was a bit emotional. Lots of things going on in my head." Nicole replied. "I appreciate it, Officer Moreno."

"No need to apologize." Moreno assured her. "And by the way, just call me Toni. Officer Moreno is too formal. We're about to go through a major hurricane together, have a feeling we'll be on first name basis sooner rather than later anyway."

"I came down here because where I live in Texas, a few years back, a hurricane was headed this way. My husband and I were preparing the property, and some of the city workers that were robotics discovered a rifle buried on our land. It wasn't being used, but it was a family heirloom. It meant a lot to my husband, and he had buried it because he didn't want to give it up, even though he knew guns weren't allowed. He argued with them and went down fighting, but they dragged him off to jail."

She sighed before continuing. "I was so mad, but I knew the kids wouldn't want me to go to jail, too, so I went to bond him out, but I wasn't able to do so till the next day. I was so worried with the storm coming. I went the next day to the jail because I had tried everything the day before and gotten nowhere, and they were loading the bus with the prisoners to evacuate. I saw him on it, and he didn't look good at all. They loaded him onto the bus, and I went to plead with the guards to let me get him before they took him. They wouldn't let me.

"They got a few miles down the road, and I saw the bus stop. I heard the robotic driver say, 'Human is deceased. Cause of death: heart attack. Probability of revival is zero percent. Risk for disease to other passengers exceeds the need to bury human. Discard human until further notice; a medical team will remove the body soon.'

"I ran to him, and I tried to revive him. I waited and waited for a medical car. None came. So, I did what any good wife would do—I drug his lifeless body home and buried him. Thankfully, we lived only a mile from the jail, but it was the hardest task I've ever done in my life, both emotionally and physically. So I don't know why I'm so emotional about a school office when I've dealt with so much worse…"

"Oh, Nicole, that's awful," Toni said softly. "The lack of humanity our society has descended into is unbelievable."

"That's not even the end of it. I was sitting by his homemade grave, bawling, when the medical cars did finally show up. They came along with security bots—I was arrested for illegally disposing of a body. The irony of that, huh?" Nicole's ending question was more of a statement.

"Oh my goodness…" Toni looked truly sympathetic for her plight.

"They put me on a bus to the evacuee prison, where I remained until the end of the storm. Upon return, my kids and I have secretly been planning to move to Alaska or Mexico, but Mexico seems to be the best bet. We were going to take our chances with the border guards around the Rio Grande, but they didn't know I was going to just distract them so my kids and grandbabies could live. I guess the universe had a different plan, huh?"

"Nicole, that's horrible. I am so, so sorry that happened to you."

"He was a good man, Clark was. He was a hard drinker when we first married, but he quit, and even through this government takeover stuff he remained sober. But that rifle was something he couldn't let go. He felt like a failure because he couldn't fight the government. I never saw him as anything but a success, and he was my best friend, my partner, and I miss him so much still. If you don't mind my asking, what happened to your family?"

The two were almost back to the locker rooms. Thunder shook the building, and lightning flashed so brightly, it lit up the entire gym floor.

"I had a wife and a daughter," Toni began. "My daughter was born in the midst of all this change. She was eight years old when the second pandemic hit hard. She and her mother got very sick, but the hospitals wouldn't even take them in because they hadn't been vaccinated for it.

"The pandemic had just started. They hadn't had time to get a shot even if they'd wanted to, and her mom didn't—she was very much against unresearched medicine. I had to get one eventually because of being in law enforcement, but her mom was very much a believer that the Earth had everything we needed to heal. However, modern medicine would and could have helped them had they been allowed to be admitted to the hospital."

He sighed, then continued. "That was when they were piloting the AI nurse and doctor program, and we got nowhere. I was sent home with them, and we were quarantined and guarded to make sure we didn't infect anyone. I wasn't even sick. They even took our dog and put it down because they believed dogs could be carriers…that made Lily even more upset. Lily was my sweet girl." He paused.

Nicole gently touched his arm. "I'm so sorry."

"She never recovered. Her mom was so sick, too. They did deliver medications to us, but only over-the-counter ones that didn't do much good. I begged and pleaded for a doctor—a human doctor—to talk to me, to call them out the things they needed, but no one cared. Lily died first, and it killed her mother seeing her die. She didn't last but another day.

"Because they were considered 'infected,' they were removed from the house and burned. I was guarded, and while I was fighting mad, my grief just overtook me. I didn't do anything for a month. Their ashes were sent to me. I was finally allowed to leave my house and resume my duties as an officer, but by then, the robotic officers were taking over. I decided to play along, believing someday I could change things. I felt like a failure to my country and my family, but then I met a Mexican man named Juan Gonzales one day while walking to work—I chose not to use my car—and we were able to talk a little bit about Mexico without being overheard, surprisingly. I have a little more authority to go incognito since I'm a law enforcement officer, so I used it to my benefit. He told me about the community in Mexico, how they are self-sustaining and preparing to come help Texas fight to become independent from the United States of the Greater World. He said Texas has been a country before, and they can do it again."

The two had already arrived at the locker rooms, realizing that they had kept talking for almost fifteen minutes before the others realized they were there.

"Hey, Officer Moreno, Nicole!" Coach Hoffner motioned for them to come meet him. "We're getting showers organized. Ladies first, so you go ahead—the others are already in there. There's plenty of showers in that locker room. I'll be right out here to keep anyone else out. I don't know how much longer we're gonna have power, either, so hurry!"

Two hours later, everyone was clean and ready for bed. They knew they had one more day of peace: it would soon be Monday, and the storm was supposed to hit early Tuesday morning. Monday would just be a day of thunderstorms and rainbands that preceded the powerful hurricane. The winds were already howling.

CHAPTER 18

LOVE AND THE GHOST OF LAKESIDE HIGH

"Someone should keep watch on those cameras through the night just in case. Who wants to take the first shift?" Moreno asked.

"I'll do it," David volunteered. "Come on, son, you too."

"Seriously, Dad?" Jason asked. He was sitting right next to Princess on the floor, chatting with Carson and Charlie.

"Yes," his dad replied. "Come on."

"Thank you," Kallie mouthed to him.

Princess rolled her eyes.

"Can I go, too, Dad?" Charlie Junior asked.

"Charlie, my dude, where's your shirt?" Charlie Senior asked. "And no. Why don't you hang around here, and you, me, and Princess can take the next shift?"

"I can take a shift now," Princess offered.

"No," Micah, Kallie, and Ophelia said almost simultaneously.

"Geez, why do you think I like him like that?! What do you possibly think is gonna happen in the middle of a hurricane?" Princess argued, rolling her eyes.

"Just stay here, Princess. That's final," Micah stated.

"Fine. Charlie, Ollie, Auggie, y'all wanna play Uno? I found some cards," Princess changed the subject.

"Y'all need to get some sleep. Tomorrow's going to be a long, hard day." Ophelia instructed.

"She's right. Everyone to bed," Charlie Senior agreed.

The adults made sure all the children were safely tucked away for the night while they themselves anxiously awaited whatever was to come.

While many things about the world had changed, though, one had not: teenagers still possessed the keen ability to stay awake at night for hours on end. Jason and his dad returned from their shift and awoke Charlie Senior and Charlie Junior to take over. This awoke Princess, but she lay there quietly until the shift change had been completed. David Fontenot, having exhausted himself, was promptly snoring. Princess sighed loudly.

"Pssst," she heard, seeing a small flashlight flicker at the door.

"Who's there? Who's awake?" Princess whispered. She was answered with more snores but saw another flicker. She quietly eased her way to the door and realized it was Jason, motioning for her to come with him. Curiosity got the best of her and she followed, glancing back to make sure the adults were all sleeping.

Once they were outside the room in the large gym, she whispered, "What if they see us on the security cameras?"

"They aren't even there yet. Hurry!" Jason motioned for her to follow. She followed and sat down beside him under the bleachers.

"This is super not comfortable. The floor is hard," she whispered.

"That's why I got this." He pulled a blanket down from the bleachers.

"Really?" she asked. "What do you want?"

"Just to talk. I'm just tired and can't sleep."

"Okay, fine, but if I get in trouble for this…" Her voice trailed off.

"Listen, we're maybe gonna die tomorrow. After that, we may die on the way to Mexico. Just live a little, okay? I brought something else, too."

He pulled out a book he had found while rummaging through the office on camera duty with his dad. Princess's eyes lit up.

"You really like books, huh?" he asked.

"Yeah, I do. Now, give me that blanket and flashlight so I can read!"

"'Please' would be nice," he grumbled. "And that blanket isn't just for you, Princess Peach."

"Why? Just why?" She rolled her eyes.

"Hey, you know what?" he said hesitantly.

"What's that?" Princess asked, suddenly shy.

He shined the flashlight at his face and said, "There was once a ghost in this school."

"Oh, for goodness' sake, seriously?" Princess laughed.

"Shhh—you're gonna wake it up," he whispered, moving closer to her.

"Oh, come on. You can't truly think there's a ghost here."

"Oh yeah, the ghost of Lakeside High … that's what this place used to be called back in the glory days."

"Before you had to wear flags to play football?" she asked mischievously.

"Hey, now, you're hurting the ghost's feelings! He was a football player, too, and he is very displeased with the way things are going here. In fact, I wouldn't be surprised if he isn't right behind you!"

"You're crazy," Princess said, but with a smile.

"You know, when I first met you, I thought you were kinda weird."

"Oh, that's so charming. Great start there."

A clap of thunder banged loudly, making them both jump.

"Dang it, I hope that didn't wake anyone up. They'll wonder where we are," Princess said worriedly.

"Relax. My dad and mom sleep through everything."

"Mine, too!" she laughed. "But Aunt Ophelia …"

"Would you quit worrying? Just hide under the blanket if they come in here and it'll just look like a pile of junk." Jason grinned.

"Oh, you're clever." Princess teased, rolling her eyes.

"So, uh, I meant to ask you before … do you, uh, have a boyfriend back home?"

Princess shook her head no, giving a little smile.

"Okay, cool. Just curious." Jason tried to act like he wasn't nervous.

"Well, there is this one guy I kinda like," she said.

Jason's face fell a bit, but then she moved closer to him.

"He's kind of a jerk, but he's also kind of a goofball, and he's a little obsessed with ghosts…"

Jason's eyes lit up. "Hmm, he sounds terrible."

"Yes, he is terrible, because he wakes people up in the middle of the night and leads them to haunted places …"

They moved closer, hearts beating quickly.

"We are going to be in so much trouble if they catch us." Princess smiled as she leaned forward, Jason pulling her closer and closer until their lips met.

However, Charlie Junior happened to see the whole thing on the monitor. Charlie Senior had fallen asleep but Charlie Junior jumped up at the sight, awakening his dad, but thankfully the display had switched to a different camera feed. "I'll be back, Dad, gotta pee!" he said, running off.

"Okay, man. I'm here. Be careful." Charlie Senior muttered sleepily.

"Are you two serious?!" Charlie Junior whispered from behind the bleachers when he arrived. "Eww! Okay, please stop kissing so I can talk to you!"

"Bro, what are you doing here? Aren't you supposed to be on watch?" Jason asked, pulling away from Princess reluctantly.

"I was, and then *this* popped up on the screen. And now I just had to see it in real time! Never gonna get that image out of my head… ick. And, for real, a blanket? What the heck were you planning on doing?"

"It's just cold down here, and we wanted to talk," Jason said.

"Yeah, lots of talking going on, I see," Charlie Junior said, climbing in beside them. "And cold? In September in Louisiana? That's a good one."

"For real, man?" Jason groaned.

"Charlie, do you ever wear a shirt?" Princess asked. "And why are you so sweaty again?"

"My dad didn't see—I just came to warn y'all. Here, come back with me to the sleeping area, and I'll just act like I woke y'all up. I'll cover for you if I need to. I wish I had a girl to kiss, too… come on, let's go back. I have to pee anyway, like for real." Charlie Junior said.

"Oh, Charlie, you're my favorite cousin! I hope we all survive." Princess smiled.

"Is that why y'all are making out under bleachers? You think we're gonna die? You better not break my cousin's heart, man. We may live, and in fact we probably will!" Charlie Junior's eternal optimist shined through in his comment.

"Chill, man, be cool. I'm not gonna do that to her. I actually really like her… a lot." Jason explained.

Princess blushed and giggled.

"SHHHHH!" Charlie said, motioning for them to follow him.

The three were able to navigate through the sleeping quarters and back to their area without detection, although Charlie did manage to accidentally wake up his mom and brothers briefly as he bumbled out of the room. But he had managed to save Jason and Princess from getting into any more mischief, at least for that night.

CHAPTER 19

ANTICIPATING THE CHAOS

The following day was one of the most peaceful days the group had all experienced in quite some time. There were no cell phones to distract them, no TunedIN alerts, and no robots dictating their every move. The teens and children played basketball in the gym for the first half of the morning, but not without Coach Hoffner reminding them they needed to shower before the power went off because he was not "gonna be smelling all you sweaty kids for days." The adults discussed the plan following the storm and decided they would wait until it passed to inform the children. Thus, the rest of the day would be spent relaxing and enjoying on last normal day before they faced the unknown outcome of their extravagant plan.

After discussing the next steps, the adults even joined the kids' basketball game briefly. Ophelia and Kallie both exchanged glances all day and talked privately about the change they noticed in Princess's behavior. They knew something was up, but they weren't sure how they had missed it. Suddenly, there was quite a bit of flirting going on.

They told Nicole about it, and Nicole assured them Jason was a great kid because he was like his dad.

"That's what I'm worried about, Mom," Ophelia argued. "He *is* like his dad. I've heard some really wild stories from his high school days you probably didn't even know about. I've lived here way longer than you ever were here."

"Ophelia, all teenagers are wild at times. You certainly were. You think your dad was an angel as a young man? Oh, my, that man was WILD. And he turned out to be amazing!" Nicole laughed, recalling her daughter's younger days.

"Mom, not everyone is Dad, and not everyone is the same! This is my niece we're talking about." Ophelia argued.

"And my daughter," Micah said, walking up. "What seems to be going on?"

"Oh, sweet Micah, you don't see it, do you? Watch the kids for thirty minutes and then come tell me if you don't see it." Nicole smiled. "I don't think it's anything to worry about—just young love. We may all die tomorrow, anyway."

"MOM!" Ophelia and Micah exclaimed simultaneously.

"I'm just saying, you never know what day will be your last. Let them be kids."

"Let them be kids?" Kallie asked. "In a huge school where there's millions of places to sneak off and hide and do God knows what?"

"And how would you know, Kallie?" Ophelia asked with a grin.

"Because I was a teenager, too, once." Kallie replied quietly.

"Yeah, she's not wrong. We used to go hide under the bleachers sometimes—" Micah began.

"EWWW! I don't want to know this!" Charlie Junior cried, popping up from out of nowhere.

"Charlie, where did you come from? And how long have you been listening?!" Ophelia looked startled.

"Oh, just long enough to know you think Jason and Princess have a thing going on, and that Aunt Kallie and Uncle Micah used to exchange spit under the bleachers."

"Gross!" Auggie yelled as he appeared behind Charlie Junior.

"Oh, great, Charlie, thanks a lot," Ophelia said.

Thunder boomed, and the power flickered.

"It's about time for us all to get clean again," Moreno stated. "If you've ever been through a hurricane, you know that it could be awhile before water and power come back. So, Coach, let's get everybody ready. I can feel the barometric pressure dropping—that storm is gonna roll in within the next few hours. Let's get cleaned up and eat supper."

No sooner than everyone had eaten and gotten cleaned up, the wind really started howling. It was about eight o'clock in the evening, and the rainbands from the actual storm began releasing their torrents. The power went out completely around nine o'clock Monday night. The kids gathered close to one another, huddled up in a corner, while the adults sat nearby, everyone holding their flashlights. David Fontenot sat in an old teacher's desk that remained in the locker room, put his head down flat, and immediately began snoring.

"How can he sleep through this?" Ophelia asked Jamie. "And how is he even comfortable?!"

"He sleeps through everything. He isn't that afraid of much." Jamie laughed. "I could tell you some stories from back in the day."

"Hey, why don't y'all tell us some stories from when y'all were kids, Mom and Dad?" Charlie Junior asked.

"Yeah!" Auggie and Ollie agreed excitedly.

"Sounds like fun, actually. I wanna know the craziest thing you ever did, Mrs. Ophelia," Jason said. "It seems like you probably did some wild stuff."

"I actually agree, she does seem like that type. No offense, Mrs. Ophelia," Carson agreed. He had been very quiet all day, but finally he spoke.

"Thanks a lot, boys," she said.

141

"They aren't wrong, dear," Nicole laughed and put her arm around her daughter. "You were certainly your own person, both then and now."

Stories began to be told, making the intense thunder and the howl of the wind a little less frightening for the younger kids especially.

Jason inched closer to Princess as the flashlight batteries died one by one. He grabbed her hand in the dark and she squeezed his back, but quickly pulled it away at the mention of flashlight battery changes.

"Mommy, I'm scared! It's dark," Auggie said.

Ollie curled up next to him, his big brown eyes large with fear. "Me too."

"It's okay, babies," Ophelia said. "Just let me feel around for the batteries and change one of these lights real quick."

"Hey, look, I got one!" Jason said as he swapped batteries quickly in the dark. "Boys, how about I tell you about the ghost of Lakeside High?"

"Not helpful, Jason." Ophelia shot him a warning look.

"Yes!" Auggie's eyes lit up. "Ghost stories!"

"I'm scared, nooo!" Ollie started to cry.

"Oh, he's a goofy ghost, though—he does silly things," Charlie Junior joined in, trying to make it better.

"That's right, this ghost makes silly things happen," Jason agreed.

"Yeah," Carson added. "He leaves banana peels out for the robot teachers to slip on!"

All the kids laughed.

"Thank you," Charlie Senior mouthed to Carson.

The tales of the silly schemes of the ghost continued in the dark as the wind howled and the rain pounded heavily against the walls of the gym. It was a welcome distraction. The threat of flooding was minimal, as the school had been rebuilt about forty years ago and sat atop sturdy piers, but they had seen water come up to the very bottom floor before. No one spoke of it now, though, as they all could all feel the intense fear already hanging in the room.

"Hey, did you pee on me?" Auggie asked Ollie. "Ew!"

David's head shot up too. "Who did that?"

"What are you talking about, David?" Jamie asked. "Nobody touched you, *couyon.*"

"I'm wet. It's cold," David complained.

"Did Ollie pee on you, too?" Auggie asked.

"I didn't pee on anyone!" Ollie protested.

"Maybe your water spilled," Nicole interjected. "Maybe the ghost decided it was time for you to get soaked, too."

Everyone laughed, which woke up Coach Hoffner, who had also been snoozing in the corner. "What's going on?" he bellowed.

"Nothing, you can go back to sleep," Moreno said, pointing his flashlight at the ceiling, and surprisingly, he did so immediately. "But I do think we need to switch locker rooms. It looks like this ceiling is about to start leaking heavily." No sooner had the words come out of his mouth than right beside David, a huge piece of ceiling collapsed, soaking him in water.

Everyone laughed—other than David, who still had a bit of a temper, and his nerves were frazzled from the roller coaster of events the last few days.

"You think it's funny? We're stuck here in the middle of a storm because some crazy woman started a riot at the game, and I'm just sick of everything and all of y'all's stupid plans!"

They all eyed one another, trying not to laugh because David, sopping wet, made quite a picture. Nicole, however, being one of the oldest in the room, walked toward him. She had never been afraid of anyone or anything other than Leichenberg's cousin so many years ago, and that had been a different fear altogether. She wasn't afraid of violent outbursts, angry men or women, or being in danger.

"David," she soothed. "I know you're upset. I am, too."

And as she said that, another piece of the ceiling started caving in, soaking her too.

It was just the comic relief they needed. Nicole and David both started laughing, along with everyone else.

"We're all a little tense," Moreno said, taking charge. "Let's just remain calm, and let's see if it's safe to move to the locker room next door. Remember, though, the gym has windows, so be aware of flying debris if any of those windows broke. Grab your stuff and let's make a run for it. Stay as close to the wall as you can and if you see something flying, duck." Moreno stood up. "And someone please wake up Coach again. I don't know how he's asleep again."

A shriek pierced the room. Nicole may not have been afraid of people, but snakes were a different story. She knew it was just a garter snake, and harmless, but she couldn't help it.

"Hold still." Charlie Junior popped up and grabbed the snake off of her head. It had fallen with the water from the ceiling, but it had landed where nobody could see it until just then.

"It's just a little garter snake," Jason agreed. "Give it to me, Charlie."

"Here." Charlie handed it to Jason.

"Uh, please don't put that thing near me," Carson said, backing away.

"Come on," Moreno said, motioning for everyone to come to the door. "Looks like we can make it right now. Go!"

The crew, carrying their blankets and flashlights, all followed behind, Jason still holding the snake.

"Hey, Princess," he said, popping up behind her as they walked carefully to the next locker room. "Like my pet?"

"Yeah, sure. Let me hold it," she said.

"Sure you can handle it?" he teased, thinking she would be afraid of the reptile.

"Just give it to me." She gently took the snake, then tossed it across the gym.

"Seriously?" Jason sighed. "I wanted to keep him!"

"What were you really gonna do with a snake?" Princess asked.

"Eat it," Micah said. "We coulda cooked it if we ran outta food!"

"So much like your dad ..." Nicole shook her head. "We aren't desperate enough to eat a snake just yet. There's plenty of food here."

The wind howled again, and several pieces of random debris begin flying through the gym. "HURRY!" Moreno shouted. They all picked up their pace and arrived safely in the next locker room, only to be met with yet another surprise.

"Who the heck are you, and how did you get in here?" Moreno demanded.

CHAPTER 20

THE WEATHERMAN

"Who are *you?*" asked one of the two men standing in the room. "And why are you still here?"

"Why is *he* here?" Jamie asked, pointing to one man wearing a TunedIN shirt who appeared to be Asian. "Y'all are the reason our country is RUINED!"

"Hey, hey, everyone calm down." The man put his open hands up. "I'm a weather reporter for the National News Center at TunedIN, but I lost all my equipment. I can't get ahold of anyone, and because someone hacked the system down here, me and my assistant—this is Pete Chang—are stuck here."

"And chill, bro, I'm from New York," Chang said, putting his hands in the air as well. "I had nothing to do with all this. I have the same feelings you do; I'm just as American as you guys are. I was born and raised in Queens. But there's not much left of New York after the riots…" His voice trailed off.

"Yeah, you be respectful of Pete, 'k?" the other man said. "Hey, you look familiar," he said, turning to Nicole.

"Oh my gosh!" Nicole exclaimed, recognition sparking within. "Connor! Connor Vincent!"

The two embraced and started chatting excitedly.

"Uh, 'scuse me, we kinda need to know what's going on here,"

David interrupted.

"I taught Connor years ago when I worked in Lafayette. He was in one of my very first classes!" Nicole smiled. "I loved his brilliance, and he was such a great kid."

"You say that about *all* your previous students, Mom," Micah murmured.

Howling wind drowned out any further conversation.

Moreno's arm hair stood on end as he eyed the two other men. "If you worked for TunedIN, are they tracking you?" he asked suspiciously.

"Oh, I wish," Connor sighed. "Most of our devices got lost as we scrambled out of the boat to get up here about an hour ago, the two left we need to repair. That storm is exhilarating, even if it's dangerous." The reporter's eyes lit up.

"What's wrong with you, man?" Princess asked, sounding more like a teenager than she had in a long time.

"Princess!" Kallie reprimanded.

"Well, I mean, she ain't wrong," Jason defended.

"Okay, here's the deal: I do work for TunedIN…" Connor eyed Moreno. "But first, can you get the big scary dude to stop staring at me?"

Moreno's hands hovered over the handcuffs attached to his left side.

"It's okay, Toni. I know him," Nicole assured.

"Who *don't* you know?" Jamie Fontenot asked with a bit of an accusing tone. She had felt a little left out since this strange family had barged into her life, and the tension of the situation was rising.

"Pipe down! We're gonna figure this out," Coach Hoffner scolded.

"You gonna let him talk to me like that, David?" Jamie asked, blue eyes flashing.

"That's my wife, Coach, and I don't appreciate you speaking to her like that. I'm not a kid anymore. I can kick your butt if I need to still," he said, kissing her forehead and then stepping toward Coach.

"Whoa, whoa, whoa, everyone take it down a few notches!" Pete raised his hands in a motion of surrender. "We're all tense. Please just let us explain how we got here. Then we'll see what we can figure out."

"What?!" David yelled over the howling wind. Just like that, the wind ceased, and a strange, eerie peace fell over the building.

"Is it over, Daddy?" Auggie asked.

"No, Aug-man," Charlie Senior sighed. "This is just the eye of the storm. We're not safe yet, but we do have some time to breathe."

"What's the eye of the storm?" asked Ollie.

Connor Vincent's eyes lit up, and he began to describe the eye of the storm and how storms form in great detail.

"Okay, that's all super interesting, but how did you end up here?" asked Kallie.

"Oh, that," Pete said. "Should we tell them?"

Moreno's hands reached back down for his cuffs, but he felt Nicole's hand gently on his as she nodded to let them talk first. Normally, someone interfering with his movement would have caused him great anger, but Moreno was growing to like and trust Nicole. Their moment of shared grief had created an unspoken bond that was growing deeper by the minute.

"Well, Pete, here's the deal—if they're here, they didn't make the bus to get out, and evacuation was mandatory. They also look familiar, and… oh! Hey, weren't you some of those people who got arrested at the riot the other night?"

They all exchanged glances. Nicole pulled her hand away from Moreno's arm as if to signal for him to be ready just in case.

"No, no, we're in the same situation as you are, in a way," Connor explained. "See, Pete and I have been working together for years. We met in college many years ago, and we developed our own secret language and code that no one has been able to crack. Pete's sister was arrested in one of the New York riots, and she was sent down to the border to await further trial. It was a human impersonating an officer who arrested her because she looked Chinese; he assumed she was part of the problem, and she, along with several Jewish families in the community, were 'arrested' and relocated until they could be deemed less of a threat. This was right before the Chinese takeover. And trust me, I'm as American as you are—I believe in freedom, even though it's long gone."

"What if he's just saying that?" Charlie Junior asked softly.

"Charlie!" Ophelia protested.

"He's right, though," Charlie Senior chimed in. "That's quite a story."

Pete pulled a crumpled picture out of his pocket. It was one of the last newspapers produced by what was once *The New York Times,* with a headline reading "Chinese and Jewish Americans Targeted in Riots in NYC." A girl resembling Pete stood crying in handcuffs, chaos surrounding her.

"Let me see that," Charlie Senior said.

He read the caption aloud: "Amy Chang, 22, of New York reported missing after being captured by extremist group for relocation."

"That is awful!" Ophelia said.

"I agree," Pete responded. "I know those people were trying to ensure we stayed free, but some of them got really insane with it and started just blaming all Chinese Americans and Jews because the timing of the conflict in the Middle East aligned with the second wave. Some blamed the Jewish Americans if they didn't blame the Chinese Americans. My parents' house got burned down with them in it, and graffitied with awful things accusing them of bringing diseases and robots to the US. My grandpa was in the US military and served in Afghanistan. I just don't understand it."

"Nothing about our world makes any sense anymore, but there is hope." Nicole nodded toward the kids. "That's your hope, right there. We did a horrible job leaving a decent world for you kids, and I'm sorry about my part in that, but I believe the next generation is going to do better. Right, kids?"

A heavy silence hung over the group.

"We will change the world, Mrs. Thibodeaux," Jason agreed.

"We will change the world," Carson echoed, followed by a chorus of the same sentiment.

Connor spoke up. "I was helping Pete get to Mexico because we listen in on conversations at the station, and it seems that if Amy escaped, she would have headed to Mexico. If not, they're probably holding her in a border jail, because she was deemed a threat by the Chinese regime as well since she'd been a vocal protester against our liberties being taken away.

"They send all dissenters to the border to be either deported, or... I don't know what exactly they do." His eyes were full of sadness and fear. "She was also my fiancé," lamented Connor. "I love her very much, and I haven't known for years if she's even still alive."

"Oh, Connor, I'm so sorry," Nicole sighed. Her heart filled with heaviness at the world that was left for those children she had taught years before, in her classroom so full of hope and joy. Even though she'd never set foot in a classroom again after Lakeside High had broken her spirit, she was still, at heart, a teacher. That is a gift that cannot be taken from someone, no matter how hard one tries.

She looked at her own son, daughter, and son-in-law, deeply concerned for what may await them.

"We do have a boat tied up outside, if it survives," Connor added.

"Thankfully, Pete here went to school for mechanical engineering. Anyone else know how to fix boats or engines?" There was silence.

"But I suppose they may be tracking it after the storm. They don't know about the plan I had to make sure Pete got to Mexico. I volunteered to come down here because it was a couple hours from where I grew up, and I was born around here before we moved. They thought a local weatherman would make a glowing story to 'please the people,' as everything does nowadays.

"I was going to come run some nonsense story about community and how well things were going, then those riots broke out. I also am very aware it probably wasn't a riot—I've seen what they insist are riots, and I've seen actual riots. They use those opportunities to show us we have no voice. I did hear they were going to consider you all dead within seventy-two hours, though, so basically . . . we have seventy-two hours to figure out how to get away," Connor explained.

"But what does it matter if we're considered dead?" David asked.

"Because being considered dead means they're going to make *sure* you are. They'll give some story about how you died, but you'll end up in a border jail, too, or worse, they'll just shoot you. I've listened and learned enough from my time at TunedIN. I worked there pretending I agreed with it all, playing the game, but I have got to find my fiancée. She's considered dead as well and is listed as deceased, but I have to know for sure. I have to know what they did with her, what they did to her."

"And I have to as well. That's my sister," Pete added.

The silence in the air hung heavy. "Let's go see how bad the flooding is outside and try to secure the boat before the eye passes," Connor finally said.

"Hey, did you ask if someone here could work on computers?" Carson asked. "I was the one who disabled all the robots. I can help with your boat." The boy had decided to trust Connor.

The weather reporter roared laughing. "My man!" he said, slapping Carson's back. "You are a genius, and brave. That is a risky, risky move, but genius!"

"We were just trying to get rid of the robot teachers. That's literally all we wanted to do," Jason added. "Then all this happened. Nothing about our plan worked."

"But don't you see—what was your name, kid?" Connor asked.

"Jason." Jason replied, looking confused.

"Jason, don't you see? The plan is even better now! You have the power to help so many people, and Carson is going to be able to disable even more of them once we get to Mexico. I'm assuming that's where the rest of you are headed, too, since you probably don't want to be 'considered dead' for real?" Connor asked.

"Mexico was the plan, but what about your fiancée?" Moreno answered.

"Pete and I are going to take a boat as far as the border of Mexico and walk to the border to see if we can scope it out and make a plan."

"You know they've got, like, horrible devices to keep people from getting in and out, right?" asked Nicole.

"There's one section near Del City that's going to be hit hard by another storm in the next week or two, or so we hope. We plan to use that, just like you're all using this storm. I've been mapping it out, and if it comes, it looks like we have a good chance of another big storm."

"If you need to use my land in Del City, I can give you the coordinates," Nicole offered.

"How are we gonna navigate past all those stupid windmills in the Gulf?" Charlie asked.

"Do not fear—those will fall today. The sustained winds are going to take them out. They aren't going to last, so any tracking technology on them will be down temporarily," Connor explained.

"You're so smart," Princess said, in awe. "How do you know all those things?"

"He's a nerd," Jason said, a little jealous of the complete amazement Princess had for this guy, even though he was clearly three times her age.

"Jason!" Jamie scolded. "You are friends with a 'nerd' that saved all of our butts."

"Thanks a lot, Mrs. Jamie," Carson laughed.

"Alright, let's go see what we can do about that boat. I'll need all the men and boys to come help—no, not you, Auggie and Ollie. You need to stay back and protect Mom, okay?" Charlie Senior winked at them.

"Okay, we'll protect her," Auggie said, kicking and punching at the air.

About an hour had passed since the boys and men left and the winds were picking up again. The women and kids walked into the gym, which had small puddles spread across the floor in several areas. There were pieces of debris lying about, and an occasional snake slithered by as they walked out of the room to see quite a sight.

"David, what... ?!" Jamie cried.

Nicole began to laugh, as she did when she was both nervous and amused.

CHAPTER 21

SICKENING NEWS

"A boat in the gym!" Ollie giggled.

The men had not only repaired the boat, but they had managed to pry down the gym doors, already weak due to the strong winds, and were attempting to push the boat inside the gym.

"It won't blow away like this!" Jason hollered. "It'll be safer inside!"

"Jason, be careful!" Princess called out.

"I'm always careful," he said, pretending to fall off the side of the boat, only to jump back up quickly as a large alligator floated past.

Carson roared with laughter. "You deserved that, man."

"Boys, hurry up and help! We don't need nobody being alligator food today," Coach barked.

"Alright, alright, we're helping," Jason replied, returning to his post of steering the boat in.

The women shook their heads.

"It's actually a pretty good idea," Ophelia commented.

"You saw that gator, huh? We're gonna have to secure the doors again once we get this boat in." David shouted.

"All those stupid showers we took really didn't help much, huh?" Charlie Junior joked, sniffing his own armpit.

"Charlie, you're getting a shower right now," Carson said, as

Charlie was, once again, shirtless.

"Just toss that boy some soap and the rain'll clean him right up," Coach laughed.

"Alright, ready, set, pull!" Moreno motioned for the other men to help him. "Charlie, you and Carson hop off the boat so it weighs a little less. We got this, come on."

After about twenty minutes of awkward maneuvering, the boat at last sat inside the gym.

"Can we take a break before we fix the doors?" Charlie Junior asked, panting.

"Well, I would say yes, but we don't have much time," Moreno said, pointing to the sky, his footing a little off.

"You okay, man?" Pete asked.

"Yeah, yeah, just dehydrated. We need to work fast, though."

"He's right," Connor replied. "The eye is almost past. The second half of the storm will be here soon. We have to work fast! I know you're tired, but if we all work together, we can do it."

"How can we help?" Jamie called.

"Y'all come over here, and you can help with the doors. But Ollie, Auggie, y'all keep guard of the boat, okay?" Charlie Senior directed.

"Okay!" the boys yelled as they climbed on the boat and began playing sword fight.

"Thankfully they're taking it well," Ophelia said as she, Kallie, and Jamie headed for the door.

"They're not as much to handle as Princess. I wish she'd worry less about that boy and more about surviving this," Kallie commented.

"What's wrong with my boy?" Jamie Fontenot asked, having also noticed what was happening.

"Nothing! They're just young, and this is a really intense situation without them making it more complicated," Kallie sighed.

"Mom!" Princess complained as she overheard, catching up to the ladies. "What are you even talking about? I'm helping!"

"I know, sweetie. We're all just a little tense." Kallie put her hand on Princess's head. "You're dad's little princess, and we just want to make sure you're safe. We should have never let you come with Grandma."

"You were eventually going to end up in a situation like this, like it or not," Nicole snapped. "You and Micah pretend the world is fine, but it's not. It's not fine at all. This is a good wake-up call for you two. I love my sweet baby boy, but I cannot believe you two just ignore the world. Princess knows more about what's happening around her than you two do! This is what the world looks like now. Have you both forgotten so fast what happened to Dad?"

"It's because of what happened to Dad that I wanted to keep her away from all this!" Micah yelled.

"Yelling isn't going to help anyone. Let's all just take a deep breath, take five, and come back in a minute," Ophelia said, ever the peacemaker. "We both miss Dad, Micah. I know it hurts." She hugged her brother, who had always looked up to her with respect.

"Ophelia, I just miss him so much...I don't know what to do without him." Micah buried his head in Ophelia's shoulder.

Princess's eyes filled with tears, too, and Jason reached to embrace her. Kallie went to stop it, but Jamie and Nicole gently touched her arms. "She needs him right now. Let it be," Nicole said.

David, ever the comedian, came up behind Jamie and poked her sides. "I guess it's mushy 'let's all hug' time," he joked.

"Come on, all of you!" Connor Vincent motioned to bring everyone close. "We all need a hug, a big group hug. Come on, little fellows!"

The winds picked up speed as lightning flashed across the sky, and for the first time in a long time, a large group of humans stood together, embracing one another tightly—some strangers, some old friends, but all with the deep hunger for connection that had been absent from society for so long. Even Coach Hoffner, who had never been much for human contact, halfheartedly joined in, cracking a little smile.

It was a magical five minutes of connection as tears flowed from the tension and adrenaline built up from the intense last few days. A crash sounded, and a small shark hit the glass of one of the gym windows. "Sharknado says it's time to get these doors secure," Charlie Senior said, and everyone laughed. "Alright, back to work, guys!"

Once the doors had been secured as best as could be expected, they all headed back to the one locker room that remained dry as the winds picked back up and lightning flashed. No words could describe the harrowing sound of the hurricane's heavy-handed howls that echoed through what was now, they assumed, early Tuesday morning.

"Let's get settled in for the last half and get some rest," Moreno suggested.

No one said much, as everyone, even Ollie and Auggie, felt the exhaustion creeping in from the last several days. They all settled into the room, flashlights in hand, and hunkered down until the storm subsided—which, with not having any access to technology, meant they had no idea if it would last hours more or days. There had been some storms that stalled and dumped rain and winds over areas for days in the past, but this one was not supposed to be that type of storm, Connor assured them.

Connor Vincent was an incredibly talented weatherman, and because he was also somewhat of a collector, he carried old-fashioned weather predicting tools with him in a display on his boat. He was using them to the best of his ability, and though he warned the others the readings wouldn't be perfect, they would be close if he combined his knowledge and his expertise with the readings.

He had brought some mechanisms into the room and was diligently working by the light of a flashlight held by his ever-present companion, Pete Chang. The children and teenagers watched with fascination, asking questions about the old equipment and patiently waiting for answers between claps of thunder and the eerie howl of the wind.

Moreno sat in the corner, away from everyone else, and stifled a cough.

Nicole, who had been right beside the kids as Connor demonstrated his vast knowledge, noticed Moreno looking worse for wear. She quietly walked over and sat beside him.

"Nicole, don't come any closer," he warned quietly. "I don't want to worry the others, and you don't need this. *We* don't need this... I can't believe the timing."

Nicole ignored his demands and gently sat down beside him. She felt his forehead and their eyes met, and she knew he already knew.

"When did you start noticing?" she asked.

"I was perfectly fine until late last night. I felt a little off this morning, but I was tired. Then, when we were out moving the boat, I almost passed out while you were inside. Told them I just felt weak from dehydration and needed more water, but I knew." Toni sighed.

"You had a shot, though, right? Not that it matters if that's what it is..." Her voice trailed off.

"You don't need to be exposed. You shouldn't be so close," Toni whispered as quietly as possible. The other adults had also been fascinated by the weather equipment and failed to notice the conversation happening in the corner.

"I've already been exposed, remember?" she said quietly.

He remembered their moment of shared grief under the desk.

"Oh, Nicole, I'm so sorry." He put his head in his hands. "I had no idea I was coming down with this."

"Don't be sorry. You had no way to know. Is that why you've been avoiding people getting near you all day?"

He nodded through real tears as memories of his wife and daughter, helpless in their own home, flashed through his mind.

"I'm sure they have test kits somewhere in the school—every school has them. I'll go get one, but I'll have to find some reason for them to let us out. You have keys to the nurse's office?" she asked.

He nodded. "I have all the keys here. I was part of the human security sometimes when the robots would malfunction. But Nicole, you don't need to risk going out there! Besides, I know where it is."

"What if you pass out?" she asked. "I'm coming with you. You saved us—you aren't going to die alone! I'm old. If I die, I die."

"Nicole, I'm not young, either." He smiled a little. "It'll be okay. You have the boat now."

"And I can't get on that boat with my kids and grandkids and all those people if I'm sick, too. Plus, they have medicine for emergencies that we'll need to get for them before the storm destroys it anyway. The parents down here could sign for their kids to have permission to get treatments from the school. Things are very different than they once were..."

They both fell silent.

"Look, they're preoccupied. Come on." Nicole helped Toni up and they slipped out of the room, unnoticed for about ten minutes.

They stepped into the gym to see there were now several inches of water seeping in, as the storm surge had reached the very bottom of the stilts upon which the school sat.

"This way," Toni motioned, ducking as a piece of debris flew through the gym. He grabbed Nicole's hand and they headed for the hallway.

"Distract me—I need a good story. Why did you quit teaching?

You seem like you're really good with kids, and you care a lot about others," Toni said, letting go of her hand as they entered the hallway.

Nicole hesitated.

"I'm sorry. You can just tell me a joke, or nothing at all! It's fine."

"No, it's okay. Well, remember how I said I knew Leichenberg's cousin?" she began, following close behind him in the long hallway.

"Yeah." Toni nodded.

"I started teaching here after several years of being an English teacher at different schools, and I was so excited. The principal who hired me wasn't Leichenberg. Her name was Macie LeBlanc, and she was phenomenal. She was the perfect balance of strict and fun, and she led with passion and energy."

"What happened?" Toni asked, pointing for her to turn.

"I actually know where to go, too. I spent many hours in this building many, many years ago," she replied. "Well, it wasn't necessarily a bad thing—Macie got pregnant, but she had some complications. The baby was fine, but she had to be hospitalized for the second half of the year. So, they pulled Leichenberg, who already wasn't a favorite, into her position because she had been teaching there for almost forty years. She was the math teacher at the time, so they had to find a new math teacher to replace her, but she knew the right people."

Nicole sighed, then continued.

"She had an entirely different outlook on education than Mrs. LeBlanc. She had also been horrible to me back when I was in her class in high school, but she didn't teach me math; she was a history teacher back then. She hated me because I was smarter than her daughter, and I always won academic awards that she felt her daughter deserved. Had she been doing the hiring, I probably wouldn't have been hired in the first place. I was reluctant to work at the same school as her, but I figured since she was in a completely different department, I'd be fine." Nicole began to recall the events of the past. "When Macie had to be hospitalized, Leichenberg was the last person I thought would be chosen as her replacement. Unfortunately for me, she was, and the kids had a hard time, too. It was culture shock for the teachers and kids alike, but there was no getting rid of her, as she was the niece of a powerful sheriff back then. That was before the war ..."

"What exactly did she do to you as an adult?" Toni asked.

"Well, the first time she came to my classroom to observe me, she didn't like anything I did. She fussed at me later because I'd used purple markers for my objectives. Another teacher got in trouble because he allowed the kids to watch a movie the day before the break. He was her replacement math teacher—he quit after a month. I spilled water on the floor in the office once where we were the other night, and she treated me like a child about it. I finally got tired of it, and I walked out."

"She was mad about purple ink?" Toni laughed. "That's hilarious. Who cares?"

"The kids always liked the purple," Nicole said passionately.

"That explains the other Leichenberg," he added.

"Oh, I think they both have some major issues. Pretty sure both are alcoholics, and that they didn't feel confident in themselves. However, I almost let that year ruin my life. I thought about running my car into a tree...but I had Ophelia and Micah to think about, and of course, Clark." Nicole hung her head, trying to put that memory out of her mind. "I'm still not proud of that."

"That bad, huh? I don't think anyone really realizes what people go through. I thought about ending it all after my wife and daughter died. I felt like I had failed them because not enough of us had stood against the government slowly taking our freedoms, but after seeing some kids walking to school the next day, escorted by robots, I decided to fight until the end, or my death would have been in vain." Toni sympathized.

"I can relate to that," Nicole sighed. "I taught some of those kids that are now adults in there, and this is not the world I envisioned for them. I'm glad you didn't end it, and I'm also glad I didn't run into that tree. Hey, this isn't the way to the nurse's office!" Nicole said.

"We have a detour to make." Toni grinned, then a cough shook his body.

"What? Toni, you okay?" Nicole asked with concern in her voice.

"I'll live," he replied. "Maybe."

"Oh, stop it," she said. "Let's get to the medicine."

"Hold on," he said, jingling his keys. "Hold the flashlight."

"Why are we in the art room?" Nicole asked. "It doesn't look like anyone's even used the art room in years."

"They haven't. It was deemed an unnecessary subject, but they never had a chance to clean it out. It's just sat here for years. What's a little toxic paint when I'm gonna die anyway?" Toni joked.

"Oh, quit it! You aren't going to die if I can help it," she said. "Why do we need paint?"

"To paint something in this building purple, of course." Toni grinned. "It's become a bucket list item for me since you think I'm about to kick the bucket anyway."

She laughed a real laugh for the first time in many years.

"Did you just snort?" he chuckled, and they both laughed even harder.

CHAPTER 22

ACCESS DENIED

"What in the world are you two doing?" David Fontenot asked from behind them.

"David! What are YOU doing?" Nicole asked.

"We noticed you two weren't there, and I volunteered to go find you. You left a muddy footprint trail—it wasn't hard to find. Wait, were y'all wanting some privacy?" He winked.

"No, nothing like that," Toni said. "Just don't come closer, David."

"Mmhmm, then why in the world are you two in here?" he yelled over the howling wind. "David, I need you to listen and not freak out, please!" Nicole hollered back, jumping to the side as a piece of the ceiling fell in.

"Found it!" Toni yelled.

"Found what?" David asked, looking thoroughly confused, then saw the purple paint. "You two came down here in the middle of a hurricane for PURPLE PAINT?!"

"David, David! Listen to me!" Nicole hollered. "David, he's sick, and I'm probably coming down with it too. We just decided to have a little fun before we died in this storm or of his sickness!"

"Hey, you used to love writing in purple until that other Leichenberg woman told you not to!" David laughed.

"How did you know about that?" Nicole asked.

"Everyone knew what was happening, but they were all divided on what to do. I liked the purple. After you left, I wrote in purple on purpose just to irritate her." David grinned mischievously, looking like the young school boy he'd been when she was his teacher.

"David, we probably have Covid Omega. Moreno most likely does. You need to go back to everyone else so you don't catch it. We were headed to get medicine and a test."

"Looks like you were getting paint," David pointed out.

"Well, we were gonna live a little first," Toni laughed.

Another piece of the ceiling fell, and a rat squeaked as it came down.

"Ick, I'm out! Rats are worse than snakes," Nicole said, jumping up and running to the door. "David, go back to your family. Tell my family we're having to quarantine."

A cough shook Toni's body again, and he began to shiver.

"Toni, let's get you to the medicine. David, please, for my family's sake, please go back. And get there safely!" Nicole urged.

"I told you there were rats in that ceiling," David said as he walked back down the hall.

Nicole shook her head. "Boys never really grow up, do they?"

"I did," Toni said, shivering.

Nicole looked at him, then at the purple paint.

"Point taken," Toni laughed, followed by a little cough.

"He used to tell me horror stories about rats falling from the ceiling, and I never believed him." Nicole explained. "I had no idea there actually were things in the ceiling. I guess that remodel didn't take care of everything!"

They both chuckled, but an even more powerful cough shook Toni's body this time. "Come on, let's get to the nurse's office so we can see what's going on." Nicole suggested.

"Alright, but grab that paintbrush I dropped. We ARE going to paint something purple before we are done," Toni said, winking.

"Clark would have liked you." Nicole sighed and laughed a little.

"He sounds like he was a good man," Toni said, patting her back.

"He was... okay, let's get to that medicine." Nicole said determinedly.

A surprise awaited them in the nurse's office, though. Two robotic nurses appeared to be operational still, though only one seemed to be on.

"How did that happen?" Nicole wondered.

"Please state your objective," the robotic nurse droned. "Security breach detected—notify authorities immediately."

Nicole and Toni exchanged looks of horror.

"It's the middle of a hurricane? Who's gonna come anyway?" Toni tried reassuring Nicole, followed by a coughing fit.

"Sit down, Toni! We'll figure it out." Nicole gently guided Toni to a chair in the nurse's office.

"Covid Omega symptoms detected," the nurse stated. "You must quarantine to avoid further exposure of fellow humans in the building."

"It's just us—two humans in the building. No others present." Toni cleared his throat and reached for the medicine cabinet.

"I detect that you are lying. Assessing that there are at least ten more humans in the vicinity."

"How did she not get deactivated?" Nicole wondered.

"Medical personnel have been left behind at any location that may harbor fugitives. Fugitives will be arrested after the storm passes." The robot responded, clearly comprehending Nicole's question.

"Oh, great," she said. "So much for buying us time."

"They can't get here if the roads are impassable, Nicole." Toni encouraged her.

"Security officers will arrive after the storm subsides and the airport is cleared for landing, and prisoners will be sent out by bus to a more secure evacuation location." The robotic and eerily human-like nurse stated.

"Oh no," Nicole said. "We have to warn the others."

"But we're sick. Let me just smash her," Toni said, grabbing a piece of debris.

"Wait, let's let it help us first!" Nicole winked. "Please examine patient for Covid Omega and assess treatment plan," she ordered.

"Please step forward for more accurate analysis." The robot requested.

Toni complied.

"Patient's blood pressure and vital signs are indicative of Covid Omega. A more conclusive analysis will be done after analyzing a blood sample. Please give me your arm."

Toni complied, and a needle appeared out of the robotic hand that appeared so deceptively human.

Five minutes later, the robot beeped. "Test results complete: Patient has Covid Omega. Treatment should begin immediately. Vaccination status: Vaccinated. Proceed with treatment."

"Treatment location?" Nicole asked.

"The Covid treatment is located in the back cabinet to the left. I will administer the dosage, which is a ten milligram vial."

Nicole retrieved the medicine and the robotic nurse then administered the medication to Toni, who was only getting weaker by the minute, now sweating profusely.

"Thank you. Second patient needs a Covid Omega test. Please test me, too." Nicole requested.

"Testing patient number two." the robot complied.

Five minutes passed, and the results concluded that Nicole, too, had contracted the virus.

"Early stages detected—two options for treatment. Would you like a shot or a pill?" the robot droned.

"I don't care. A shot." Nicole shrugged, not really that concerned as her symptoms were not really starting to develop yet, it seemed.

"Error: Unable to give either. Blood work reveals you have not received an initial vaccination. Chances for survival are less than three percent due to past medical history of asthma and severe allergic reactions."

Toni, despite being weak and exhausted, lifted his head. "Tell me where the medicine is!" he demanded. "She *will* get the medicine."

"Request denied. Access to medication is limited to those who have received initial vaccination, and those with a chance of survival greater than eighty percent." The robotic nurse refused to comply with Toni's demands.

Toni headed toward the medicine cabinet.

"Sir, you are not authorized to access the medication. Security breach noted for the arrival of troops upon the storm's end."

"We have got to warn the others," Nicole said.

"There's an old intercom in the office I bet still works," Toni said through labored breath.

"Hey, you, step away from the medicine cabinet!" Jamie Fontenot appeared in the doorway along with Connor.

"What are you two doing here?" Toni asked.

"Well, David told us y'all weren't doing so hot. Connor insisted on coming down here, but I wouldn't let David come down again. He's making sure the others can handle the kids. It's getting pretty rough in the locker room, but the gym is starting to flood even more."

"Give me a minute," Connor said, stepping behind the robot. "Nurse, deactivate due to security breach in coding."

"No security breach detected," the robotic nurse responded.

Connor stepped closer. "Nurse, code nine."

"Code … nine…" Connor repeated, and the robot began to shut down partially.

And from behind, Connor grabbed the robot's neck with a rope he had brought from the boat and pulled as hard as he could. "Damage to robot assessed. Code nine."

The nurse robot continued to short out. "Ccc-ccc-code … nine…" it repeated a few times before its head exploded.

"That's a trick I learned a long time ago. If someone suspects that a robot's been reprogrammed to go against the government, it's a code nine, and once you tell them that they shut off. It's not common knowledge, and they change the code now and then."

"Then why did you strangle it?" Nicole asked.

"'Cause I've always wanted to strangle one of those stupid machines, and I finally had a chance without going to jail for it." Connor said flatly, not intending to be humorous, but it still made everyone laugh.

Toni laughed so hard, he coughed more.

"Get her medication, please. You don't have to touch her, but it's in that cabinet." He pointed across the room and Connor grabbed it.

"Can you even give it to her in your condition?" he asked Toni.

"Toss me that shot," Nicole said. "I've been giving myself shots for years because I have asthma, although I haven't had one in years. They won't give them to me anymore since I'm not vaccinated. That's why this sickness is kicking my butt so hard—it's been years since I've had what I really need."

She scoffed before she continued. "I have some 'illegal' herbal medication I use that helps. It's nothing that should be illegal at all, but you know how even growing tomatoes is illegal now? Yeah, well, I have herbal remedies for my asthma I hide on my land in Del Mar. So, I have no problem giving myself shots. Clark, on the other hand…Toni, you don't pass out at the sight of a shot being given, do you?"

"No, why?" Toni asked.

"Oh, okay, good," she said, jabbing her arm. "Connor, go back and warn everyone there are still medical robots activated and they're sending robotic troops here right after the storm. Now GET OUT! Tell my family I love them, but they cannot go to Mexico with Covid Omega. I've lived a good life—Toni and I will be fine. We'll try to meet y'all eventually if we recover. Get out as fast as you can."

"But Mrs. Thibodeaux, we aren't gonna leave you!" Connor argued.

"She's right, Connor. We're sick. The chances of us even making it with this are low, and then when they put us in jail ..." Toni's voice trailed off. "We will cover for y'all, though. I promise."

"Please tell my babies and grandbabies I love them very much," Nicole said, tears flowing down her face.

"We will," Jamie assured her. "Thank you for helping our son when we were in jail. I'll never forget you, Mrs. Thibodeaux." She wiped a tear from her eyes.

Connor started toward Nicole to wrap her in a hug, but she stopped him. "Connor, I need you to go save the day—you cannot get sick. David, Charlie Senior, and Micah, along with Coach, are all good guys. Pete needs you, too. He needs you to find Amy. You need to find out what happened to her. Please look out for Princess... she's my special girl. And make sure those kiddos all are safe. Can you do that for me?"

"I can do that." Connor nodded, holding back tears.

"Go!" she said as the thunder crashed.

Connor and Jamie dashed out of the room.

CHAPTER 23

PURPLE REBELLION

"So, what are we painting purple?" Toni asked, pulling the paint bucket to his side.

"We really don't need to," she said. "You're so weak."

"I want to. Let's go paint the town purple! We need to get to the office anyway to see if we can spot any more hidden robots on those cameras, if they're even still working."

"You need to rest. Here, take this water bottle. Drink some and take a little nap. Look, can you get up on this cot?" Nicole asked.

Toni nodded, too weak to argue.

"I'm not as sick as you, and I got the medication thanks to you. I may be okay after all. But you are burning up," she said. "I wonder if there's any ice packs in the fridge that are still halfway cold."

"Nicole," he murmured. "I am so sorry. You didn't deserve this."

"Shhh, you just lie down, and I'll get you taken care of. We don't always get what we deserve, good or bad. Life is just life—you roll with the punches as best you can."

"You're a good woman," he said with a warm smile.

"And you are delirious with fever," she replied, gently helping Toni lay his head down. "I'm gonna dig through the fridge and find something cold for you. And this vest is too heavy for your chest right now—let's get that off."

Nicole gently removed his vest and shirt, placed some ice packs from the fridge that were still relatively cool over his chest and on his forehead, and sat beside the cot, mind racing and head beginning to pound. Not long after, she fell asleep curled up in a blanket, her head full of dark black hair streaked with silver resting on a chair beside the cot. The two dozed peacefully, awaiting their potentially tragic fate.

A loud crash awakened Toni and Nicole as they were dozing about forty-five minutes after the medication had taken effect. The medication was powerful, and though not without side effects, the US president at the time Hallie Randolph—the second woman in history to become president—had convinced the country to trade much of its freedom for the powerful anecdote that China offered for good reason.

The second pandemic, known as the Omega Outbreak or the Second Wave, had claimed more lives than the first pandemic and all the following strains combined. It was a super strain of Covid that had mutated to become almost immune to treatment. Most of the country knew by that point that it was biological warfare, as a third of the world population had been destroyed by the Omega Outbreak, and those who had not soon became casualties of the extreme riots and protests about how the world leaders were handling the new pandemic. Without treatment, though, the new strain was a death sentence.

Extremist groups from both sides had been silenced as the United States of the Greater World was given an ultimatum from the United Nations, under which they were now governed: Comply, or your cities will be destroyed. Those who refused to accept a vaccination would not be treated under this decree and would be isolated until their certain death. Unless they were at home, in which case they would be forcibly removed by robotic health care workers, and at the end of the pandemic, their ashes would be mailed back to their families.

Many suspected that the robotic initiative to relieve health care workers was a ruse to mask the fact that those infected were being given lethal injections. A story had been leaked about it, but it had been immediately squelched by TunedIN as a "false narrative" and "dangerous rhetoric." That was in the early stages of the pandemic, and as it progressed and more and more artificial intelligence took over various jobs, less and less human touch was added. At some point it progressed to a simple letter—if the families even received that—detailing that the bodies were being used for scientific research, and because they had refused to be hospitalized or vaccinated, they would be used for more research to help develop a cure.

The antidote, called Alphatrox, was developed soon after. The "thank you" cards received by families were a huge source of anger and incited more riots. Despite the heavily divided country, the disease still raged, and it was undeniable that Alphatrox was indeed effective. Had the Constitution not been rewritten, perhaps the legality of many of these practices would have been questioned. Had doctors been primarily human, not robotic, perhaps an element of compassion would have shone through the darkness. But to protect health care workers, artificial intelligence had slowly replaced them.

While humans still were present in some aspects of health care, it had become almost entirely robotic, partly due to the absolute devastation and loss that had overwhelmed humanity. The few Americans who remembered the United States as it once was were silenced in one way or another, and unfortunately for the older generation of millennials, they had not prepared their children and grandchildren for the world to come.

"Wow, that stuff works well," Toni commented, ice packs falling from his chest as he sat up and stretched.

Nicole, however, though she had received some relief, seemed to be worsening. She was covered in sweat, and her breath was labored as she motioned she needed water, a coughing fit shaking her entire body.

"Nicole?" Toni grabbed her as she fell forward, then gently placed her on the cot, handing her a water bottle that she seemed too weak to even hold. He motioned for her to lift her head and held her chin up while she drank.

"Why..." she began, "is it not working? It's... supposed... to be... the best."

"Maybe the dosage wasn't enough," Toni said, worried.

Just as he did, the other robot in the room activated, and they sensed the storm had passed.

"Must... act fast," she rasped, pointing at the purple paint.

"Nicole, that isn't important right now," Toni said. "That was just a silly idea. You have to rest."

"No," she said, regaining her strength a little. "Get Connor, but don't get near him. Please tell him I need his recording equipment they were fixing earlier, and I need him to get my family to safety. I am not going to make it, and it's okay." She wheezed and wiped sweat from her brow.

"I've always hated being sweaty," she chuckled a little. "Ironic I'd die sweating. I hope there's no sweat in heaven."

"Nicole, you are gonna be okay." Toni eyed the now reactivated robot.

"Medical care needs detected in surviving fugitives," the robot droned.

"Code nine!" Toni yelled, but the robot remained active. "CODE NINE!"

Nothing.

"They must have changed it. Probably after they detected that one," Toni said, pointing at the decapitated robotic nurse. He approached the robot slowly and held out his hand. "Assess treatment needed," he commanded.

"Assessing treatment… Covid Omega detected in bloodstream, but Alphatrox has begun to work. Patient will recover in approximately seventy-two hours."

A snap and click awoke Nicole, who had dozed off again briefly as her body fought the powerful virus with all its might.

"What in the world, Toni?" Nicole looked amused, but a little surprised at what she saw before her that had transpired in the few moments while she had fallen back asleep.

Toni grinned a little. The robot stood with its arms tied back in handcuffs.

"You are performing an illegal function. Blood type has been matched. Antonio Moreno, sheriff deputy of the Southwest Louisiana Coastal Region, has been relieved of duties and will be arrested soon."

"Shut up. I should have done this a long time ago." Toni grabbed the rope from the floor and pulled as hard as he could until the robot started to stutter and beep. He then kicked the machine and pushed it out the door, sending it into the slowly rising water.

"The good news is, it'll be a little while before they can find us because the flood risk will be too great," he said. "Nicole, I can't leave you like this."

"Please," she said, grabbing the water and regaining more strength. "I need you to find Connor. He will know why I need what I need. Tell him Mrs. Thibodeaux needs to do a weather report before she dies. He can also say his equipment was stolen if he gets caught.

"Tell my grandbabies and my babies I love them. Tell Charlie Robert that I love him like my own kids, and that I am going to make a better world for them. Tell Kallie to go easy on Jason, and to give the kid a chance. Tell Jason if he breaks my grandbaby's heart, I'll come back to haunt him forever, and tell David I always believed in him and he needs to work with Connor to save my family. Tell him his wife is amazing, and tell them all I'm so sorry that we left this world the mess it is."

"Nicole, you're gonna be okay," Toni said, grabbing another shot from the cabinet. "Here. It can't hurt, right?"

"Okay, why not?" she agreed, holding out her arm. "Glad this doesn't make you pass out," she laughed.

"I cannot leave you," he sighed.

"Toni, listen to me," she said, standing up. "Give me that paint and get back as fast as you can."

"Yes, ma'am, Mrs. Thibodeaux." He saluted. "I see why those kids liked you so much." Tears welled in his eyes, but he quickly turned to exit the room, the water level hitting a little over his ankles.

"I may have to swim, but I'll be back," he promised.

Toni did make it to the rest of the crew, although there were some new faces. He quickly explained Nicole's dying wishes to Connor, who complied quickly, knowing there must be a good reason.

"I'm sorry I had to come back and risk infecting y'all. Nicole and I did find treatments in there, though," he said. "But hers didn't work."

Connor and Pete gave one another a sad look. "They only work if they've been vaccinated. They made the cure that way on purpose," Pete said.

"How do you know that?" Toni asked.

"TunedIN. We keep track of 'false narratives,' and it's been hard keeping our mouths shut, but we had no hope of finding Amy if we leaked it. Plus, who believes stuff like that anymore anyway? No one would have believed us."

He sighed.

The McGinnis family gathered around the Thibodeaux family, all of their eyes welling with tears. "We want to see her," Charlie Senior said.

"But she said for you not to go!" Toni argued.

"We'll risk it," Ophelia said. "Please. Plus, if we're going to survive that plague, we need to go grab some shots from that office in case we do get it."

"Okay, but just a little heads-up, there's a decapitated robot in there. Try not to touch it and get shocked," Toni said dryly.

David Fontenot threw back his head and howled with laughter. "Dude, you are the best. Too bad Mrs. Thibodeaux's not gonna make it—you'd be perfect for her."

"David!" Jamie scolded, eyeing the others.

Thankfully, though, Nicole's entire family had a great sense of humor, and the moment proved to be comedic relief needed as everyone laughed.

"Okay, well, let's get this show on the road! Bunch of *couyons,* the lot of you, but I wouldn't wanna be stuck in no hurricane with anyone else," Coach Hoffner's voice boomed. "Y'all get outta here, hurry!"

"Okay, let's go, kids."David said quietly.

"Wait, why are they back?" Toni asked, pointing to the new adult and three more teens, one of whom was a severely injured JoJo.

"We'll explain later," Connor said. "Let's just get to Mrs. Thibodeaux."

"Mind if I go, too?" Jason asked.

"This is for their family, son," Jamie said.

"No, it's okay. She took care of him while y'all were in jail. I bet she'd be happy to say goodbye, but I don't want him to get infected. Unless y'all want to come get shots, too? Because I'm guessing you haven't gotten them either?" Charlie Senior questioned.

"Nope, sure haven't, and we'll take our chances. But Jason, you got the shot because they wouldn't let you in the school without it, but you still can get sick," David said. "You're gonna be eighteen soon. You'll be making a lot more adult decisions than I ever dreamed soon, because I hate to tell you, but college is probably not in the cards anymore. It's up to you."

"I understand," he agreed. "Hey, where's Carson?"

"Don't worry about that right now, please," Princess pleaded. "Why don't you just stay here, Jason? I don't want you to get sick."

"She saved our lives. I'm going. I won't breathe—look!" Jason pulled his shirt over his mouth and nose. "See, I'm good."

Princess smiled a little and squeezed his hand, leading him forward as they both joined the rest of the family venturing out.

"That kid turned out a lot better than I was at his age," David mused as he watched his son walk through the now ankle-deep water with the crew behind Connor.

Meanwhile, Nicole was busy in the nurse's office. She had just finished her work of art when she saw a familiar face. He stumbled in, not noticing her, and headed straight for the medication cabinet, fumbling around frantically.

"Carson?" Nicole asked weakly.

"Oh Mrs. Thibodeaux, I didn't see you there," he said, hanging his head.

"Carson," she said gently. "What are you doing here?"

"I... uh . . . think I'm sick," he mumbled.

"Carson, what are you really doing here?" she asked as another coughing fit shook her body.

"Oh, Mrs. Thibodeaux..." He sighed and began to sob. "It's all my fault! You're dying, everyone is in danger, my parents have no idea if I'm dead or alive, and my friend JoJo is gonna die, too! Little Jo was such a great kid with so much potential . . ."

"Wait, whoa, slow down! JoJo evacuated with Mrs. Jayla, though." Nicole looked confused.

"No, they never made it out. Even Leichenberg is dead—not that I care that much, but I never meant for anyone to die. I'm better off just not…" His voice trailed off.

"Living?" Nicole asked compassionately.

"What's the point? Nothing we do ever matters," he sighed, grabbing a pill bottle he had found.

"Carson, listen to me. Everything you do matters. Look at this wall. Why do you think I'd do this on my deathbed?"

Carson shrugged.

"There was a time I believed nothing I did would matter, either. I had the same thoughts as you. It was very different, but I felt like I had failed everyone and everything. I was on my second career failure, right after finally making progress to make more income for my household. Everyone was proud of me, then I did something stupid, and they weren't." Nicole recalled.

Carson's eyes widened.

"Oh, nothing illegal or horrible—just said some dumb stuff to the wrong people and argued about how to make things better, but instead I just made life worse for myself and everyone else." She sighed wistfully. "But you know what, Carson? It all worked out. I had to live, because this moment that's about to happen is what I was born for. I was born to die for others, apparently," she half-heartedly chuckled.

"But what made you decide to live?" Carson asked. "And… if you don't mind me asking…"

"Go ahead, ask me anything, sweetie. Honesty is one thing I have never lacked." She smiled. "Glad that second dose seems to be helping. I feel more strength now."

"Second dose? How much medicine did Officer Moreno give you?" Carson asked, looking concerned.

"Oh, don't worry. It's not going to work anyway; I already figured that out. It's just helping the symptoms briefly. But anyway …" Nicole continued.

"Oh…did you, um…try?" Carson asked quietly. "And if so… how?"

"I thought about it, Carson. I truly did. It was more of a fleeting thought, but it intensified. Once I was driving to meet Clark after a horrendous day at work, and I felt like such a huge failure. I didn't have either of the kids with me, and I sped up as fast as my car would go down that backroad, just hoping that I'd lose control. I've never driven that fast in my life, and that was before electric cars, so it was fast, like a-hundred-twenty-miles-per-hour fast. *Fast* fast."

Carson couldn't help but laugh, imagining this woman driving that fast down a backroad. "For real?"

"Yeah, and you know what stopped me?" Nicole asked.

He shook his head.

"I'll make it fast, because I hear people coming that I told not to come," she sighed. "Just like their mama, that bunch. They don't listen." She chuckled a little.

"What kept you going?" Carson asked.

"I knew that I had Ophelia and Micah to live for, and I knew Clark would never survive if I didn't live. I knew Clark knew that I struggled with severe anxiety, and he would always wonder if it had truly been an accident. I knew it would have sent him over the edge. But I was in a dark, dark place. I saw the faces of about one hundred students who would have been devastated to lose a teacher to death in the middle of the year, and I also knew that I didn't want any of them following suit. I knew I had to be strong," she paused before continuing her recollection.

"While I did eventually quit before the end of the year, at least those students didn't have to go to a funeral. I never would have wanted my kids or those kids to have to endure that. I knew I had some purpose, something bigger than myself. I just never knew what it was until this moment, right before my death. The death date that is coming today is the day I was meant to die."

"But Mrs. Thibodeaux, those ADULTS in there respect you as well as the kids. You are amazing! I don't understand why you would think otherwise," Carson said.

"Carson, amazing people don't always escape from things like anxiety or suicidal thoughts. In fact, you never know what someone else is going through. I had to tell myself that about the other Leichenberg years ago—I had no idea what kind of pain she was going through. I was just mad for a long time, but I wasn't gonna let that kill me." Her gaze intensified. "Carson, look at me. You are an amazing person, too. You are strong, smart, and I see something special in you, young man. Please promise me you'll remember that?" she pleaded.

"Yes, ma'am," he said, slowly capping the bottle and placing it back in its spot.

"Before you close that cabinet, got anything for headaches?"

Carson laughed. "Here," he said as he tossed her a bottle of aspirin.

"Thanks." Nicole smiled. "You ARE an amazing kid, you know that?"

"She says that to every kid!" a voice called from outside the door.

"Charlie Junior, don't you dare come in here!" she yelled with raspy breath.

"Carson?" Charlie Junior asked, hearing his voice. "What are you doing in here?"

"He got caught in the water and all turned around in the dark, but he's fine." Nicole winked at him.

"Thanks," he mouthed to her, thankful she saved him having to explain himself.

"Oh my God," Jason said, laughing as he entered. "Bruh, this is awesome!"

"What is it?" Ophelia asked, pushing closer.

The door swung open, and the rest of them saw what Jason had witnessed first.

In bright purple paint, on the wall of the nurse's office was written:

OBJECTIVE: MAKE AMERICA FREE AGAIN.

WE THE PEOPLE OF THE UNITED STATES OF AMERICA, IN ORDER TO FORM A MORE PERFECT UNION, ESTABLISH JUSTICE, ENSURE DOMESTIC TRANQUILITY, PROVIDE FOR THE COMMON DEFENSE, PROMOTE THE GENERAL WELFARE, AND SECURE THE BLESSINGS OF LIBERTY TO OURSELVES AND OUR POSTERITY, DO ORDAIN AND ESTABLISH THIS CONSTITUTION FOR THE UNITED STATES OF AMERICA.

LIFE, LIBERTY, THE PURSUIT OF HAPPINESS. WE WANT IT BACK.

—NICOLE THIBODEAUX
(THIS IS MY LAST ACT OF DEFIANCE.)

"I told you not to come!" Nicole scolded Charlie Senior, Ophelia, Micah, and Kallie.

"Mom!" Micah ran to her. "Oh my goodness, you're so sick."

"Grandma!" Ollie and Augie yelled, running to her before Ophelia could stop them.

"Have you all had shots?" she asked.

"I have," Kallie said.

"Same," Micah said.

"They made me get it." Princess rolled her eyes.

"Good. Grab those Alphatrox doses for if you do get sick—it'll save you. Use two or three, because the ones they have here in the schools are just enough to ease symptoms until you can get a real dose, but the real dose is around three of the small ones." Nicole explained.

"Mom, how do you know this?" Micah asked. "And why won't it save you?"

"Because it's my time, sweetie," she answered. "I love you all very much. Ophelia, did you wanna go ahead and give it to your boys?"

"They made us get them shots to enroll them in school, so we'll just grab some injectors for if they do get sick. The Fontenots work from home, so they've been able to avoid getting a shot, but they kept getting random fines. That's probably why they immediately went for them at the football game," Ophelia reasoned.

"Yeah, probably so," Charlie Senior agreed.

Sirens began blaring, and the faint sound of a helicopter could be heard several miles away.

"Hurry up, Connor, I need to do this! First, come here and let me tell you all goodbye. Just don't get too close," Nicole instructed. "Jason, why are you here, too? I don't want you to get sick."

"Because I wanted to be here, and you helped me, and...." He looked down a little.

"I know." Nicole nodded. "Be good to her. Did you get my message?"

"Yes, ma'am. I promise not to make you haunt me." He grinned.

"He's a little scared of ghosts," Princess said as she grinned too.

"Good. His dad certainly wasn't afraid enough of them," Nicole laughed.

"Okay, here's what you wanted, Mrs. T." Connor placed the tools near her. "And Mrs. Thibodeaux?"

"Yes?" she asked.

"Thank you for everything." Connor grabbed her and squeezed her in a big hug, despite her protests that he would get sick.

Tears filled her eyes as she gave one last hug to each member of her family, and then she motioned for them to go with Connor.

"Hurry! You won't get far if you don't go now," she urged. "Toni, please go with them."

"No. I'm staying here with you, Nicole, whatever happens," responded Toni, who had been hanging in the background while she said her goodbyes. "A police officer will be a welcome presence in your little rebellion to those who still secretly want just that." He pointed to the wall. "We have to keep trying to get that back, and I'm not leaving you to die alone. Even if I die, too."

"But—" she began.

"I insist," he said as he sat down in the chair beside her.

"Ready?" she asked him, pressing the buttons Connor had instructed her to press before he had left with her family.

With the press of a few buttons, TunedIN experienced one of the first major hacks in over a decade. Connor Vincent was a genius and, combined with Pete Chang, an undetected powerful force.

Millions of viewers watched as Nicole and Toni made their simple plea to the people of the United States of the Greater World:

"Make America Free Again."

"Americans, I am dying of this awful plague. They are LYING to you. Alphatrox only works if you are vaccinated. I am living proof," she wheezed.

"This man lost his family to the Omega virus, and what did he get in return for years of serving his country? Two small boxes of ashes—not even a choice of how his loved ones were laid to rest! This is what you get when you sell your freedom!" Nicole's voice was passionate. "Death, chaos, heartache…"

"This woman is a passionate soul, a wonderful person who saved multiple people, including CHILDREN that your stupid artificial intelligence agents left to die in a jail before a major hurricane! The blood of MILLIONS is on your hands. My wife, and my daughter … were refused medical treatment, cremated against my will…"

Toni's voice trailed off as Nicole grabbed his hand. Slowly, she began to recite the first words of the preamble to the original Constitution.

"We the people…"

He wiped a tear from his eyes and squeezed her hand, joining her.

"Of the United States of AMERICA…"

The executives at TunedIN were frantically trying to stop the broadcast, but the message had been heard.

Just as the two reached "the Blessings of Liberty," all screens went black around the nation, and an emergency message was broadcast to the entire country:

Stolen equipment detected in the Coastal Region of Southwest Louisiana. Former Officer Antonio Moreno is assumed armed and dangerous, charged with inciting riots, disturbing the peace, and now is wanted for crimes of treason against the United States of the Greater World. Nicole Thibodeaux of San Antonio, Texas, once a teacher at the very school where the accomplices are taking shelter, is also wanted for similar charges.

Any means necessary will be used to eliminate the danger they pose to society. Several minors and adults remain missing in the aftermath of Hurricane Camden; among them are believed to be our own Connor Vincent and Pete Chang. The equipment used in the illegal broadcast just minutes ago has been determined to have been stolen from Vincent's boat, and while there is no sign of Vincent, Chang, or the boat, it is believed these TunedIN reporters were killed by Antonio Moreno and Nicole Thibodeaux. All persons are guilty until proven innocent.

Please disregard the violent nature of their message. All riots and protests will, as usual, be subject to persecution to the full extent of the law. Your safety is our number one priority in the United States of the Greater World.

Nicole and Toni, hand in hand, stood firmly as the helicopters landed with a loud thud on top of the building. They heard the announcement still blasting from the loudspeaker of the helicopter as the sound of broken glass and clanging metal echoed through the school. Robots equipped with aquatic protection stormed into the building.

"Place your hands in the air," an armed robotic soldier instructed.

"We are live with the coverage of two wanted criminals," said Taylor Trenton, the reporter, standing close behind the robots.

Nicole's cough began to shake her body, and the camera quickly cut to Toni's face. "This is what you've done to us!" he yelled.

"Place your hands in the air, or deadly force will be utilized," one of the robots droned.

Nicole, still weak, grabbed Toni's hand. She looked at him, then at the robots with defiance. "We the people, of the United States…"

Toni joined her, his deep voice resounding as they spoke in unison.

"HOOAH!" he yelled as he watched the gun aimed directly at him fire a shot that pierced his chest, his last words a battle cry.

"TONI!" Nicole dropped to the floor beside him, crying.

"Woman appears to have symptoms of dehydration and sickness impairing judgment. Hold your fire," a medic robot instructed.

"Former Officer Antonio Moreno has been detained and has

suffered a deadly blow!" Taylor Trenton reported excitedly. This could possibly be just the big break she needed to become a respected reporter. "Nicole Thibodeaux, the other suspect, appears to be suffering from dehydration and perhaps the Omega virus and is mentally incapable of making good judgments. This could change everything if the virus proves to be the cause of her erratic behavior. Could she be exonerated?"

"Erratic behavior?" Nicole raised an eyebrow, weakly lifting her head from the floor.

"Mrs. Thibodeaux, can you hear us?" the reporter asked, pointing the microphone at her.

"Yes, I can. Please reassess my mental state, because I am perfectly fine. I am in my right mind, and I would do it all again in a heartbeat. This was a good man, my friend, that YOU, the country he served, killed!"

"CUT! Stop filming, you'll make it worse!" the director yelled into Taylor's earpiece. "Make it like she's crazy—that's our only angle. Mentally unstable due to the virus. She can still serve our cause, though. Like she mentioned, she didn't have the right treatment. Give her the Alphatrox injector, and make sure you film it."

"Oh, yeah! That'll help her snap out of it, hopefully," Taylor agreed. "Give her the Alphatrox injector," she instructed the medics.

"Commander, Alphatrox injector activator has been requested. Permission to inject the patient?" the robot asked.

"Permission granted," a gruff human voice came from the loudspeaker of the helicopter.

"Taylor, you give it to her. It'll make for a better story," the director said.

"Copy that," the human commander replied. "Give injector to Taylor and allow her to inject the patient."

"Injection transferred to human," the medic robot complied.

"Mrs. Thibodeaux, please relax your arm. We are going to help you," Taylor said, sitting beside her. "We are live again, giving Nicole Thibodeaux the Alphatrox injector to help relieve her symptoms and hopefully restore her mental faculties!"

Taylor smiled at the camera.

Splashes of purple completely obscured the camera lens, followed by a shriek of disgust and a hearty laugh from Nicole Thibodeaux before the needle injected into her arm silenced her forever.